# What's Going On at ardvark?

# What's Going On at UAardvark?

Lawrence S. Wittner

**Solidarity Press**

Second Edition, December 2014

*What's Going On at UAardvark?* is a work of fiction.

To order additional copies of this title, contact your favorite local bookstore or visit www.LawrenceSWittner.com.

Book and cover design by Rita Petithory.

Author photo by Allen Ballard.

Second edition prepared for publication by Steve Wickham.

Published by Solidarity Press.

Printed in the United States of America.

ISBN: 978-0-69226-1125

# Books by Lawrence S. Wittner

*Nonfiction:*

Rebels Against War

Cold War America

American Intervention in Greece, 1943-1949

One World or None

Resisting the Bomb

Toward Nuclear Abolition

Confronting the Bomb

Working for Peace and Justice

*Fiction:*

What's Going On at UAardvark?

*To all who believe that the pursuit of knowledge
is not a commercial venture*

# Contents

# Preface to the Second Edition

I wrote this novel as a satire on modern trends in higher education and, more generally, in American life. Therefore, tap-tap-tapping away on my trusty keyboard in an effort to produce amusing, colorful sketches, I tried to make my characters as bizarre as possible. Yet, when it comes to bizarre behavior on college and university campuses—or, for that matter, in the United States—how can a writer possibly stay ahead of the curve?

Let me give you an example. The central theme of *What's Going On at UAardvark?* is the corporatization of higher education, and I thought this novel provided some pretty zany material along these lines. But, in the spring of 2013, a very short time after the book's publication, I discovered that the reality was even more outlandish than I had imagined. At that time, New York Governor Andrew Cuomo announced, with great fanfare, his Tax-Free New York plan. Under it, most SUNY campuses, some private colleges, and zones adjacent to SUNY campuses would be thrown open to private, profit-making companies—businesses that would be exempted from state taxes on sales, property, the income of their owners, and the income of their employees for a period of ten years. Faculty, Cuomo said, would have to "get interested and participate in entrepreneurial activities." This corporate welfare scheme (re-named Start-Up New York) sailed through the state legislature in the closing days of its 2013 session. Consequently, this tax giveaway to the wealthy and overprivileged now supplements New York State's $7 billion in annual gifts to private businesses that promise to increase employment (but somehow never do). What value this university-business partnership has for higher education remains to be seen.

A similar love fest is shaping up on campuses elsewhere in the nation. The University of Wisconsin was designed as a "laboratory of democracy," which would improve the education, health, and well-being of the people of that state. But, in recent years, that university has experienced severe state budget cuts, thus setting it on a very different path—one toward a devil's bargain with big business. Departments are increasingly relying on grants and corporations for their revenue. And he who pays the piper calls the tune. Thanks to a $100,000 gift from MillerCoors (the beer company), the university's Department of Bacteriology now has a "fermentation lab" to research... beer-making! And more of the same will soon be under way. Jeff Immelt, the CEO of General Electric (which not so long ago bragged that it brought "good things to life" while dumping 1.3 million pounds of toxic PCBs into the Hudson River), recently told the University of Wisconsin's Board of Regents that the university must become a "strategic partner" with private businesses through its research, funding priorities, and workforce.

With partners like these, who needs enemies?

Meanwhile, on college and university campuses across the United States, government funding for education is being slashed, the salaries of administrators are soaring into the millions, the number of administrators proliferate into the godzillions, and once middle class faculty are turned into impoverished, rootless adjuncts, applying for (and receiving) food stamps. At the same time, liberal arts education is being replaced by narrow vocational training, classes that once brought faculty and students together for face-to-face discussions are replaced by massive, on-line courses, football and other games are fanatically promoted, and student tuition soars into the stratosphere. Corporations are thriving, but the pursuit and diffusion of knowledge are dying.

All of this is enough to make one think that higher education is thoroughly out of line with American life—at least until one takes a look at American life. Dominated by greedy corporate hucksters, rightwing politicians, fundamentalist fanatics, mindless mass media, and gun-toting, self-anointed saviors of the nation, it has become so profoundly regressive and bizarre that I will forgo discussing it here at length. Suffice it to say that, as Henry Adams once suggested in another context, the overall direction of American life might well disprove Darwin's theory of evolution.

Anyway, against this backdrop of the collapse of what used to be called Western civilization, I hope we can still get some good laughs out of *What's Going On at UAardvark?* We can certainly use them!

Albany, New York                                    Lawrence S. Wittner
December 15, 2014

All their cares, hopes, joys, affections, virtues, and associations seemed to be melted down into dollars.

Charles Dickens, *Martin Chuzzlewit*


Thought is subversive and revolutionary . . . merciless to privilege, established institutions, and comfortable habit . . . . Thought is great and swift and free.

Bertrand Russell, *Principles of Social Reconstruction*

# Memorandum #367

From: The Bureau of Knowledge

To: All Learners

Re: Educational Reform on the Backward Planet ("Earth")

Date: 6 Helios 31,058

If you have studied the history of the solar system, you might be familiar with aspects of the upheaval that began at UAardvark and gradually swept across much of the Backward Planet ("Earth") in the year 31,055—what the inhabitants of that unruly celestial body call the early 21$^{st}$ century.

At the time, we Vartanians were paying very little attention to developments in the Earthians' educational system, for we were preoccupied with trying to prevent them from slaughtering one another through wars and destroying their habitat through mindless consumption of resources—practices that they had perfected without acquiring more useful social skills. Unfortunately, they were relatively primitive creatures, and we did not have the resources to attend to their many problems simultaneously.

Nevertheless, when developments at UAardvark sparked a revolt with significant consequences, we immediately assigned a team of specialists on the Backward Planet to gather the necessary materials and put together a report on that upheaval. Using our sophisticated monitoring devices, we had been taping the activities and thoughts of the Earthians for many years, and this served our specialists well in assembling the necessary data.

Given the peculiar customs and practices of the Earthians,

we decided to entrust the drafting of the final report to an Earthian, as only she could fully comprehend the data and write the story in a fashion consistent with their unique thought patterns and culture. This employment of a native Earthian is quite unusual, of course, for under normal circumstances we scrupulously avoid calling attention to ourselves. But, in this case, the activities of the Earthians were so extraordinary—even suggesting some measure of social progress—that we thought an exception was warranted.

The resulting story—*What's Going On at UAardvark?*—is the latest of our popular Knowledge Expanders, and you are welcome to absorb it via your mental audio/video receivers.

We wish you many pleasant hours while you augment your understanding of these exasperating but, in some ways, appealing creatures.

# Chapter 1

## The Unraveling of Jake Holland

Jake Holland was thoroughly demoralized. In fact, early that April, lying in bed, he was not even sure he was still alive.

While the late morning sun crept through the holes in his bedroom window shades, Jake rose slowly from the depths of sleep with a terrible hangover. Its source remained mysterious, but its reality could not be denied. Amid the throbbing pain, he gradually managed to roll over to a sitting position and place his feet, one after the other, on the floor. "If I had a wife any longer," he mused, "she might have greeted me with 'Good morning!'" But, for better or worse, he didn't. "Probably better," he thought. "It's certainly not a good morning!"

As he headed toward the bathroom, he steadied himself along the way by placing one hand on the wall. Finally, reaching the sink, he turned the faucet and splashed cold water on his face. Swallowing three aspirin, he stared for a long time at his bloodshot eyes in the mirror. Jake was a tall, well-built man, but his body was definitely going to seed. It certainly ached, particularly his head. "There have been better days," he concluded. "Much better days."

Jake was professor of English at UAardvark, a public university in Aardvark, Indiana, and had once had a very promising academic career. In the wake of discovering dozens of previously unpublished, quite revealing letters by Jack London, Jake had become a renowned expert on that novelist's life and literary works. This was a specialty that suited him well, for like the socialist London, Jake had leftwing views and believed, more or less, in the historic mission of the working class to build a new society. At the least, Jake was venomously hostile to corporate power and contemptuous of the mindless consumerism that it spawned. For years, his meat and potatoes course dealt with the Naturalist writers of the early twentieth century: Theodore Dreiser, Frank Norris, and London—all sharp social critics. To the horror of the administration and many of his more elitist colleagues, Jake strode about town and the campus clad in dungarees, an old flannel shirt, an ancient pair of combat boots, and, when the weather grew colder, a raggedy mackinaw.

For roughly 15 years, Jake had also been a zealous political activist. When earlier campus administrations sought to make deals with corporations, he fought them to a standstill. When antiwar demonstrations rocked the campus, Jake led them. When administrators mistreated faculty, Jake rallied his colleagues to the defense of their fellow workers. For some time, he contributed a weekly column—"Our Moronic Masters"—to the campus and town newspapers, mocking not only UAardvark administrators, but also state and national officials. Campus presidents would surely have fired Jake had it not been for the difficulties they might have had with the campus union, in which, naturally, Jake played a role.

However, the rightward trends of the past decade had sapped his fighting spirit. Despite his best efforts, corporations gained greater and greater influence on the campus, in the state, and in the nation. The town newspaper, the *Aardvark Enterprise,* decided to replace his weekly column with one focused on athletics at the local junior high school. UAardvark students grew increasingly conventional and cynical. And the campus union, in which he had once placed great hopes, came under the control of shallow, self-interested individuals.

Gradually, Jake learned to drown his political hopes and dreams in alcohol. Sitting in his armchair brooding, with a glass of whiskey in his hand, he took a vacation from research and writing, stopped attending demonstrations and political events, and on occasion failed to show up to teach his classes. Meanwhile, his wife of 10 years—who did not appreciate this descent into depression and alcoholism—left him to join a commune in California. Now a committed lesbian and massage therapist with her own TV program, she sent him a postcard every once in a while, asking about his health. With nothing positive to report, he ultimately stopped replying. During the last year, especially, although he still felt in control of the situation, never a day passed when he did not turn to a bottle of Jack Daniels for comfort.

Despite his slow degeneration, however, Jake remained in many ways an interesting, engaging individual. Bright, amusing, offbeat, and handsome in a rugged way, Jake still managed to attract women into his life. Indeed, in the years after his wife's departure, several women faculty members and a small number of women graduate students had affairs with him. But none lasted very long. He was too much of a burnt-out case—a wreck of the hardworking scholar and political activist that he had once been—to appeal to them on a long-term basis.

So here he was at 50 years of age, staggering unsteadily downstairs, wondering if he had anything in the house that he could drink (aside from whiskey) or eat (when had he last eaten?) to get him through another grim day at UAardvark. Entering the kitchen, he saw plenty of dirty glasses, empty bottles, and grimy plates, but found nothing in the refrigerator except the remains of some cheese, an old loaf of bread, and the last dregs of a jar of instant coffee. "My *yiddishe momme* would have been horrified," he grunted. Although not at all interested in religion, Jake knew his long-deceased Jewish mother had had much higher standards for *her* kitchen!

He filled a kettle at the sink, placed it carefully on the stove, and lit the burner. "So far so good," he told himself, feeling his spirits begin to lift.

But, then, heading toward the kitchen table, he banged his knee sharply against the neighboring chair. Cursing softly, he slumped down onto it. Eventually, when the pain subsided, he arose again to open the refrigerator and explore the food issue. Not good. The cheese was dry and hard, while the bread had large green mold covering portions of its surface.

"Well, it could be worse," he reasoned. "Rush Limbaugh might be joining me for breakfast." Using the only clean knife, he chiseled away some hard chips from the cheese and, then, turning to the bread, cut away the moldy sections. "I'll save these for Rush," he muttered. Then, pouring a cup of instant coffee for himself, he combined the remainder of the bread with the cheese and took a stab at what passed for breakfast. It was terrible. No, this definitely wasn't a good morning.

As his head cleared a bit with the impact of the coffee, he had an even more disconcerting thought. He was supposed to be teaching a class in . . . 20 minutes! And what was the subject? Damned if he remembered. Storing the last of the bread and cheese in the refrigerator, he concluded that there was no time to prepare for the class or even to go rummaging in his files for something that might do for lecture notes. Instead, he'd wing it, as he had done so many times in recent years. Grabbing his jacket and a stack of crumpled student midterm exams, he rushed out the door.

As Jake drove toward UAardvark, he thought about the students in his class. Would any of them have done the reading? Even if they had, he harbored little hope for a useful discussion. The only student who appeared to have an inquiring mind was that young woman with purple hair and a ring through her eyebrow. What was her name? Randall! Natasha Randall. She seemed genuinely interested in the course, at least more than most students were.

When he arrived on campus, he edged out a colleague's car in a short-lived battle to secure an available parking space and stumbled up the stairs of his classroom building. Weaving his way down its crowded halls, Jake did his best to ignore the television sets blasting away. As usual, students were standing about or sprawled on the hall floor, their jaws slack, watching rightwing demagogues and commercials. But he drove the image from his mind and plunged into his large classroom. He was only five minutes late. Good enough! He'd made it. Who said he could no longer cope?

# Chapter 2

## Springtime for Corporations

## at UAardvark

Jake's demoralization, like that of a growing number of his colleagues, largely reflected the situation at UAardvark.

If a visitor from another planet had landed on that campus that month, he might have thought that he had not arrived at a major university, but at a particularly garish shopping mall. Everywhere, bright billboards advertised an array of corporate products. Even the university buildings were covered with corporate logos and huge pictures of handsome, laughing young people driving cars, watching television, buying clothing, pressing buttons on electronic gadgets, chugging beer, and, overall, having a wonderful time as consumers. Amid the cornucopia of products, only books seemed to be missing.

Similarly, the four student dormitory quadrangles— Petroleum Quad, Insurance Quad, Finance Quad, and Pharma Quad—were each comprised of buildings devoted to corporate promotion. Petroleum Quad, for example, consisted of ExxonMobil Hall, BP Hall, Chevron Hall, and Koch Industries Hall. Given the fact that oil corporations outnumbered dormitories, some companies were left out, and felt aggrieved at this. But, after all, the winning firms had merely outbid the losing ones. If the losers wanted to, they could raise their bids for dorm contracts during the next round of bidding.

The classroom buildings, too, bore corporate names (for

example, Walmart Hall, Coca Cola Hall, and Philip Morris Hall), as did their classrooms (the Cargill Room, the Merrill Lynch Room, and the Nike Room). It cost the companies a bit more to rename entire schools, but that was also feasible, at least for a hefty price. Thus, the campus boasted the AIG School of Business, the Fox News School of Communications, the Monsanto School of Science, and the Dow Chemical School of Public Health.

To tap the resources of the local business community, the UAardvark administration let local enterprises bid for departments—or at least those that major corporations seemed unlikely to covet. As a result, there was now a Joey's Grill Department of English, a Herman's Used Cars Department of History, an Acme Liquor Store Department of Sociology, an Ajax Porta Potty Department of Philosophy, and a Hilda's Beauty Salon Department of Women's Studies.

Within dorms, class buildings, and department offices, corporate-sponsored television programs blasted away night and day. Indeed, it was a violation of university regulations to turn them off. Only the university president had a special dispensation to shut off his television set, and then only for what was defined as "crucial business."

Actually, things had not always been like this at UAardvark. In fact, when the campus was built, back in the 1960s, it even had a different name. Located in the small city of Aardvark, the school was originally called Aardvark University. But, for reasons no one outside the administration understood, the name was changed to the University at Aardvark and, ultimately, to UAardvark.

The site for the rapidly-constructed campus was a thickly wooded, hilly area on the outskirts of the city. About the only thing located on the property, aside from grass, trees, squirrels, and mosquitoes, was an aging state insane asylum, which, the faculty later joked, provided an appropriate beginning for UAardvark. In short order, the state planners of the campus, in their wisdom, had the entire area bulldozed flat one summer. As a result, the dry, packed soil, no longer held together by grass and trees, was swept up by heavy winds and blown across the area in major sandstorms, thus destroying the air conditioning units and interiors of nearby motels, restaurants, and other enterprises.

Nevertheless, despite the ensuing lawsuits, the planners moved forward with the ill-conceived project. Identical buildings were constructed in a perfectly symmetrical fashion and thin rows of trees, all of the same type and height, were also planted—both at great cost. When the first faculty and students arrived on the new campus, they were astonished at its alienating quality and bewildered in their attempts to find their way around it. No names appeared on the buildings and everything, of course, looked the same.

Gradually, however, UAardvark acquired some human touches. Grudgingly recognizing the chaos and confusion, the administration had names affixed to buildings: Social Science, Mathematics, Art, and so on. When it came time to add new buildings, they were erected in different styles. Faculty members met one another and began to gather for coffee, friendships, and flirtations. Growing ever more countercultural, students became livelier and more interesting. Soon the campus was rocked by protests against the Vietnam War, as well as against racism and sexism. Although the administration was still alarmingly aloof and, in general, remarkably clueless about intellectual life, the faculty began to push back against absurd *diktats* from the campus and state administrations. UAardvark still lacked a great deal of intellectual excitement, but it was becoming a more or less typical American university.

In certain ways, UAardvark was also a very egalitarian place. Because education there was virtually free of charge, it attracted many students from the more impoverished ranks of the state and nation—students whose parents had never been able to afford to attend college. Now they could attend, and even enroll in graduate and professional programs. UAardvark, as faculty members began to say, was "the people's university."

Starting in the 1980s, though, a steady slide began toward corporatization. One after another, Indiana's governors began to champion a policy of creating a "business-friendly" environment in the state. This meant cutting taxes for the wealthy, reducing state regulation of business activities, and slashing funding for public services. UAardvark, of course, was a public service—an expensive public service—and therefore underwent severe cutbacks in state funding. To compensate for the cutbacks, UAardvark sharply hiked its tuition. And it also began replacing full-time faculty with part-timers, paid so little that they applied for (and received) food stamps. Finally, the university commenced vigorous campaigns to attract large corporate donations. Indeed, campus presidents and other administrators were hired primarily with this goal in mind.

All of this led logically to the current campus policy of an open door for corporations. After spending $1.6 million on a "branding" campaign, the campus administration came back with a new slogan that soon appeared everywhere, on campus and off: "UAardvark: The Business-Friendly University."

Corporations loved it. Business leaders flocked to meetings with campus administrators, offering top dollar for advertising on campus, for the naming of buildings, and for an array of other, previously forbidden, services. One plan they suggested was to have faculty members set aside the last 15 minutes of every class for commercials that would appear on a large screen in the front of every classroom. Furthermore, just in case students were inclined to bolt, check their email, or text rather than watch commercial messages, faculty would test students on the information at the beginning of the following class session. "That can certainly be arranged," the administrators assured the businessmen.

Another idea suggested by the business leaders, who, above all, were "practical" men rather than "woolly-headed idealists," was to put teaching on a more businesslike basis. Why not, they asked, require faculty, when teaching, to wear jackets adorned with their corporate logo? Why not sell admission to courses? Why not even sell grades? Why not pay faculty on the basis of the number of their "customers" (their students)? Why not get rid of "frills" like language courses, philosophy, poetry, art, and music? These suggestions all made sense to the latest crop of administrators, who thought much like their business counterparts. After all, they said, wasn't education a business too? Why treat it any differently?

Thus, by that April, UAardvark was well on the way to full corporatization. Commercial influence was everywhere in evidence, and students were more cynical and complacent than in the past. Of course, given the sharply rising cost of tuition, a higher percentage of students than in earlier years came from comfortable backgrounds and had no objection to the role marked out for them as corporate managers and consumers. But this was only part of the story, for many students were simply jaded and convinced that resistance was futile. As for the faculty, the one-two punch from state and campus administrators, combined with the spreading corporate presence, had left them almost entirely demoralized.

It was springtime for corporations at UAardvark, but winter for students and faculty.

# Chapter 3

## Jake Teaches His Class

Looking about the cavernous lecture hall, Jake could see that roughly half the 250 students in the class were absent. That was about par for the course—except for a few days before an exam, when missing students suddenly materialized in hopes of getting hints about questions that might appear on it. Some students, he knew, had dropped the course, including the campus's two self-proclaimed Marxist-Leninist militants, who had decided that Jake was a "revisionist" and, therefore, that it would be counterrevolutionary to remain in his class. But most of the absentees just didn't bother to attend class sessions.

He couldn't entirely blame them, for the classroom certainly did not provide a learning-friendly environment. Lacking any windows, the hall became stiflingly hot in winter. Occasionally, dirty water dripped through a portion of the ceiling and fell, drop by maddening drop, into a large garbage can. Although a high-tech podium stood in the front corner of the room, Jake preferred to give lectures closer to the student seating area. Consequently, after numerous phone calls to assorted university bureaucrats, he managed to have a table placed there. On it rested a small university lectern. Sometimes, though, on arrival, he would discover one or both of them missing. Today it was the lectern. But he could afford to shrug off its absence on this occasion. After all, he hadn't brought any lecture notes.

What Jake had brought with him was a stack of 26 graded midterm exams that he'd been attempting to return to the relevant students for the past three weeks. All of them had been consistently absent. At the outset of the class session, he read the names of the students aloud, finding once again that none of them was present—or at least interested enough to step forward and pick up his or her exam paper. Jake wondered if they didn't care about their grades. Or if they had dropped the course. Or if they had forgotten that they were taking the course. He'd probably never know.

Shaking off these discouraging thoughts, he turned his mind to the course subject—Twentieth Century American Literature—and began the lead-in to his lecture. "Today," he said, "I'm going to provide you with some thoughts on what has been called the 'proletarian novel.' I plan to approach that issue broadly and, then, focus on two novels that you've been assigned for this course, Jack London's *The Iron Heel* and John Steinbeck's *The Grapes of Wrath*."

He looked around. Some students were writing in their notebooks, while others were typing on their laptop computers. Most, though, seemed to be texting, playing video games, talking on cell phones, or chatting with their friends in neighboring seats. In the back row, students swayed back and forth, probably in time to the music piped in through their earphones.

Although Jake didn't know it, one of his "students" worked for the university's office of the vice president for surveillance. Like numerous other employees of that office, he had been assigned to file reports on what suspicious faculty members said in class. In fact, typing away on his laptop, he was filing a report even as Jake spoke. "This dangerous perfesser," he wrote, "is a comernest or a socialite or mebbe a libral, and shud be carfully wached. He's defanitly an anti-Amerrikan." Two rows back, another university spy, whose job was to keep tabs on the surveillance program's employees, was busy filing a report about the vice president's agent.

Meanwhile, Jake pressed forward with his lecture, delivering what he considered a thought-provoking analysis of novels by, for, and about blue-collar workers in the early twentieth century. It wasn't brilliant, he realized. But, after all, he had a hangover. Finishing up in a sweat, he felt pretty good about his performance.

"Any questions?" he asked.

A big fat boy wearing earphones raised his hand and asked: "Will that, like, be on the final exam?"

"It might be," said Jake. "Everything covered in the course is grist for the mill."

A heavily made-up girl in a skin-tight tank top followed up. "Like, what *will* be on the test?"

"Well, if I told you in advance, then it wouldn't be much of an exam, would it?" Jake said, doing his best to smile politely.

But the girl was persistent. "Lots of teachers give out the questions before the exam."

Jake shrugged. "I don't."

A short boy, with bulging arm and leg muscles and wearing a baseball cap backward on his head, suggested an alternative. "How about, like, watching a TV show instead of taking the exam?"

When Jake rebuffed this appeal, as well, his action elicited groans from several of the campus athletes.

"Anyway," Jake said, "let's drop this issue of the exam, at

least for the time being, and turn to something that should be more interesting—the novel."

Some students snickered. Others resumed texting or blowing up monsters on their video games.

Taking a deep breath, Jake asked: "Do you think Steinbeck, in *The Grapes of Wrath*, used the character Jim Casey as a symbol for someone else?"

Silence reigned.

Jake tried again. "Casey is the preacher of a new religion and his initials are 'JC.' Does that remind you of anyone famous?"

Finally, one of the students hazarded a guess: "Jesus Christ?"

"Very good," said Jake, relieved that someone finally "got it." He went on to discuss the use of Christ imagery in leftwing fiction.

But the rest of the class session was tough going, largely due to a lack of student participation.

Hoping that John Ford's film version of *The Grapes of Wrath*—which he had shown in the previous class session— would spark greater discussion, Jake asked the students what they found most striking about it.

"It was, like, real old fashioned," said a homely girl between chews of gum.

"What do you mean?" asked Jake.

Before she could reply, a crew-cut boy stopped horsing around with his friend long enough to call out. "Black and white," he said. "Like, where was the color?"

Jake felt a strong impulse to strangle him. But, as a longtime teacher, he had learned the necessity of patience. So, anxious to get students engaged with the content of the story, he asked the class how the endings of the book and the film differed.

No one except Natasha Randall offered a response. But he was struck by the fact that she had it just right. "In the film," she said, "Tom Joad goes off to lead a battle for justice after Casey has raised his class consciousness. In the novel, though, the Joad family struggles on much longer." She paused a moment, then added: "The book finishes up when the family's most selfish member, Rosasharn, learns the importance of sharing."

To Jake, her answer provided a thin ray of sunshine on an otherwise dark, cloudy day.

Determined to get to the bottom of the class's sluggishness, he asked: "How many of you have read the book?" Only six students raised their hands, and he silently wondered how many members of even this small group were telling the truth.

It was tough to teach a literature course, he thought, when students didn't read the literature.

He was tempted to berate his students for their intellectual laziness. But, then, a better idea flashed through his mind. Consequently, he launched into a rather creative mini-lecture composed of fake people and events, beginning with the claim that London's novel, *The Iron Heel*, was about a fashion show.

As usual, students either took notes or went on with their other activities.

Ten minutes later, when the buzzer announced the end of the class session, he told the students that his concluding remarks were all fictitious, and that they should forget about them. "If you had done the reading, you wouldn't have been so gullible," he said. "In fact, you'd be a lot more capable of dealing with the world that confronts you."

A few students responded by crossing out the material in their notebooks or deleting it on their computer screens. But most shrugged or said, "Whatever." To judge from the amused expression on their faces, only Natasha and a few other students got the point.

As for Jake, he had a powerful craving to clear out of there and have a drink.

# Chapter 4

## Harry Anderson

Harry Anderson sat at a small table in the Scoop, a rather scruffy, off-campus coffee house, waiting impatiently for Jake's arrival. A tall, lanky, bearded professor of history, Harry was roughly Jake's age and his best friend on the faculty. He had been worried for some time about Jake's descent into alcoholism, and hoped the English teacher's lateness—though so far by only about five minutes—didn't reflect a stopover at a local bar.

But then Jake's familiar bulk burst through the coffee house door, and Harry felt an instant sense of relief, mixed with affection.

"Sorry I'm late, Harry," Jake said, settling down on a chair directly across the table from him.

"That's OK, Jake. I take it you had another exciting class?"

Jake rolled his eyes. "It's hard to describe how bad it was. If more than a handful of students had done the reading, it certainly didn't show."

Harry smiled cynically. "Are you still expecting students to read books? About all they seem to read these days are the messages they text to one another."

"Well, I'm getting used to that, I guess," said Jake, with a sigh. "But, you know, none of them seems to have the least sense of the tension that has existed between the rich and the poor. Hasn't that tension been an important part of literature? Of history? Whatever happened to the class struggle?"

"Ah, poor Jake," Harry said. "The only class struggle on their minds is the struggle to show up for their classes on campus. And an awful lot of them don't put much effort into that, either!"

Interrupted by the waitress, a pink-haired student with purple tattoos up and down her arms, they observed her sadly, wondering why she had decided to mutilate herself like this. Then they ordered coffee for both of them, a hefty sandwich for Harry, and a piece of zucchini bread for Jake—what he called, jokingly, his vegetable of the day.

Shaking his finger at Jake in reproach, Harry said: "You really ought to eat more—particularly healthy foods—and drink less."

"So my wife used to tell me," Jake said, dunking the zucchini bread in his coffee.

"Maybe you should have listened to her."

"You have a point," Jake conceded. "Perhaps I'll order another slice!" He grinned, and Harry grinned back, shaking his head in mock exasperation.

"Anyway, Harry," Jake said, changing the subject, "how does it happen that, with the state constantly cutting back on expenditures for public education, it's providing massive funding for building a new stadium for the Pitbulls?" The UAardvark Pitbulls were the campus football team, which Jake, Harry, and most of the faculty considered a useless, expensive frill at what was supposed to be an institution of higher education.

"God knows," replied Harry. "I assume that the governor considers football more important than peripheral things like teaching and research. The real question is how this university ever got stuck with a name for the team like the Pitbulls—dogs that are both ugly and vicious."

"Don't you know?" Jake asked. "Compared to other schools

with football teams, this is a relatively new one. So, when UAardvark finally got its turn to choose a mascot, the pool was very small, and didn't even include Aardvarks. I understand that some of the alternatives were the Beetles, the Hippopotami, and the Lizards."

"If that's true, it's pretty bizarre," Harry said, not quite sure whether Jake was serious or whether he was kidding. But, he reflected, it was no more bizarre than the administration's recent campaign among students for what it called Smart Sex. What was Smart Sex anyway? A commercial substitute for the good old-fashioned mingling of bodies? He shuddered at the thought, and hoped that students had enough common sense—or at least glandular secretion—to continue engaging in the same kinds of sex that had characterized the past.

Returning, though, to the issue of state aid—or, rather, the disappearance of it—Harry added: "But at least as bizarre in this time of sharp reductions in government funding is the fact that President Hopkins is hiring two more top administrators—doubtless at impressive (and undeserved) salaries."

"I hadn't heard about these new administrators," said Jake, sipping his coffee. "What are their jobs?"

"Well, one is to serve as vice president for marketing and the other is to serve as vice president for technology."

"I can understand the hiring of the marketing honcho," Jake said. "After all, everything is turning into marketing around here. The next thing you know they'll have us ringing up sales for candy and cigarettes in our classrooms. But why this technology guy?"

Harry looked at his friend in surprise. "You mean you

haven't heard about the administration's grand plan for the New Technology Center? It's all part of our esteemed president's attempt to build campus-business partnerships."

"It's hard to imagine that there could be any more of them," muttered Jake.

For a time, the two faculty members brooded on this fact.

Harry was the first to break their silence. "You know, Jake, this campus administration and its harebrained schemes would have provided wonderful material for your long-lost column in the *Aardvark Enterprise.*"

Jake nodded his head in agreement.

"It might have lasted longer if you'd changed its title to something a little less offensive to the Establishment than 'Our Moronic Masters,'" Harry said.

"Yes," Jake mused, with a renewed twinkle in his eye. "Maybe it should have been called 'Our Malevolent Masters.'"

"Or 'Our Mindless Monsters,'" added Harry, getting into the spirit of the thing.

"Wait, wait. Let's get serious about this," Jake said, meaning exactly the opposite. "If we really want to reinstate the column, it should be called something that will appeal to corporate and campus officials. How about 'Our Magnificent Moneymen'?"

Laughing until the tears streamed down their cheeks, the two friends eventually fell to reflecting on the fact that life at UAardvark, in the city of Aardvark, and in the United States was quite absurd and, even worse, that there appeared to be little that they could do about it. A few minutes later, still chuckling, they paid their check, left a generous tip for the mutilated waitress, and headed out the door.

# Chapter 5

## Two Visits

Jake always felt his spirits lift when speaking with Harry. But, as he drove homeward, the overarching gloom about his life, his work, and his times began to descend upon him once again. Passing one of his favorite haunts, the Galway Bar and Grill, he decided that he could use a drink.

The Galway was thinly inhabited this early in the day and, as usual, dimly lighted. Old-fashioned Irish ballads about the Emerald Isle played softly in the background, and this was one reason that Jake loved the place. Another was that the Irish nationalist owner, "Wild Bill" Kelly, had resisted the temptation of having a UAardvark department named after his bar. And a third was that the Galway served whiskey, which, at the moment, was just what he craved.

Settling on a barstool, Jake ordered a shot. "Just one," he swore to himself.

Wild Bill, a plump, good-natured, rumpled man who tended bar on occasion, set the drink in front of him and, with business slow at this time of day, embarked on his favorite topic of conversation: women. "I heard this one just the other day," he remarked. "Do you know what it means to come home at night to a woman who'll give you a little love, a little affection, a little tenderness?"

Jake shook his head, giving Wild Bill a green light for the punch line.

The bar owner smiled: "It means you're in the wrong house!"

Jake gave an appreciative laugh, though the joke struck him as cutting uncomfortably close to home. When Bill departed to serve another customer, Jake sipped his drink slowly, contemplating the dissolution of his marriage and the state of the universe. But these subjects did not produce many cheering thoughts. And so he turned his mind to his friend Ellen, whose image provided a far more upbeat way to greet the afternoon.

"Ellen, Ellen, Ellen," he mused. "Why do you have to be taken?"

Ellen Smithers was a 35-year-old assistant professor of women's studies at UAardvark. Some Americans viewed feminists and women's studies teachers as man-haters, but that stereotype certainly didn't fit Ellen, who got on well with women and men alike. Furthermore, although crew cut, bereft of makeup, and almost always clad in baggy jeans and male shirts, she was a very attractive young woman. Ellen also held leftwing political views and, unlike Jake, had lost none of her fighting spirit. Indeed, she was still an activist and proud of it.

To all appearances, Ellen and Jake were just friends. But deeper currents swirled under the surface. Although Jake never discussed their relationship with Ellen, he was rather infatuated with her. What Ellen thought of him was unclear, but she certainly seemed very fond of him.

Unfortunately, even if Jake was in good physical and psychological shape—which he was not—their relationship went no further, for Ellen was fanatically devoted to her husband, Frank Collins.

Frank, a partially paralyzed U.S. Army veteran, had turned vehemently antiwar, mostly based on what he had seen and learned in the armed forces. "We're only killers, fighting other killers, and massacring civilians along the way," he sometimes said. "What's the point of that?" His debilitated condition appeared to have been caused by something the Army would not discuss—perhaps contamination by depleted uranium, used by the U.S. military during the Gulf War. And yet, despite Frank's bitterness about his military experience, he was a very charming, likeable fellow.

"What a sad story all around," Jake brooded. Then, suddenly, the thought came to his mind that he'd much rather see Ellen in person than cry about her and Frank over his third drink, which had miraculously appeared despite his good intentions. (Where had the second gone?) So, downing it quickly, before it disappeared, he headed out the door and staggered a few blocks over to Ellen and Frank's house.

Surprised at Jake's unexpected appearance, Ellen let him in and seemed happy to see him. Even so, she indicated that he should keep his voice down, as Frank was sleeping. "He's had a difficult day," she explained. "He keeps passing out, but those military bastards won't tell us a thing."

"Yes, I know," said Jake. "Everything's always top secret with them—at least when it serves their interests."

"But how are you?" she asked, giving Jake a smile that dazzled him. "You haven't been drinking again, have you?" Her smile faded to a look of genuine concern.

"Well, let's just say I'm temperate," he responded with a boyish grin. "I stop when I can no longer count the number of drinks."

"Jake, you're impossible," she said, adopting a stern

expression before a more affectionate one broke through. "You really need to get off that stuff. It's going to kill you one day if you don't."

"I would get off it for the right cause," he said. "But my life is hardly worth it."

"Well, consider this cause," she said, growing more serious. "Have you heard about the New Technology Center?"

"Yes," he replied, delighted to be able to show her that he hadn't entirely abandoned his political concerns. "Harry and I were discussing it earlier today." Jake failed to add that he still knew very little about the project.

"Well, what do you think of it?" she asked.

Jake paused a bit, groping for an appropriate response. "It sounds like another scheme of the campus administration to cozy up to big business," he remarked breezily. "But I'm not sure that there's anything that anyone can do about the New Technology Center, especially when we don't know, exactly, what President Hopkins's plans *are* for it."

"But suppose we find out what those plans are, Jake?" she said, grinning mischievously in the way he loved. "Suppose I file a Freedom of Information Act request with the government and get the full story on their corporate schemes?"

Although Jake urged her not to expect too much from this plan, Ellen was irrepressible and retorted: "Jake, don't be so pessimistic! I'm sure that Hopkins and his corporate cronies are up to no good. And this is feasible!" Still dubious that she would be able to uncover anything useful, he was also wary lest she think badly of him. So he smiled benignly and heard her out.

While Ellen babbled on about the FOIA request, Jake

noticed that her eyes were alive with excitement and her face was flushed. Occasionally, her body quivered with a fierce determination. Looking on, Jake felt a warm sense of affection sweeping over him. If he weren't a burnt-out case, grown cynical over the years, he would almost call it love. "Ah, Ellen, Ellen," he thought, admiring her once again. "You are one wonderful woman!"

# Chapter 6

## Ellen Does Some Serious Thinking

With Jake's departure, Ellen tried to get her mind back to Frank and his deteriorating condition. But it was a difficult job, for she could not easily evade thinking about Jake. As she had known for some time, she found him very attractive. And she also liked him a lot.

She knew, however, that her preoccupation with Jake shouldn't carry much weight. After all, lengthy experience showed she had terrible taste in men. During her sophomore year at college, she became seriously smitten with a young, handsome sociology major, Barry, and they often stayed up late at night, talking together animatedly, making plans to change the world. But Barry, it turned out, was better at changing his politics, and by his junior year had become a business major, en route to a well-paid corporate career. Appalled, Ellen had many a tearful discussion with him about his future and the fate of the world. Then, when all else failed, she terminated the relationship.

In her senior year, she met Jon, a gentle English major who spent much of his time writing poetry, planting flowers, and smoking pot. Attracted by his soulful eyes and his long, curly hair—and also pretty sure that he'd never morph into a businessman or a rightwinger—Ellen moved in with him. To her delight, they were happy together, a situation that lasted for almost a year. But, after graduation, Jon spent more and more of his time getting stoned and less and less of it doing anything else. Eventually, to Ellen's relief, he packed his bedroll and hitchhiked to California to join an ashram, known for heightening spiritual consciousness through transcendental meditation and psychedelic drugs.

A couple of years later, during her graduate work in women's studies, Ellen met Sergio, and she knew right away that she had finally found the man for her. An intern in psychiatry, Sergio was fascinated by social pathology and the mindset that caused it. Ellen thought that was marvelous, and had great hopes for him and for their flowering relationship. One day, however, after classes, she was in their off-campus apartment, studying for an exam, when the police phoned to notify her that Sergio was in jail, having gunned down 14 doctors, nurses, and patients at his training hospital. For reasons beyond anyone's understanding, all of the victims were redheads. Even though Ellen's hair was blondish brown, she decided that the time had come to break things off with Sergio.

About the only man who hadn't disappointed her was Frank. Since his experience in the Gulf War, he had consistently challenged what they both viewed as the ridiculous, flag-waving, militarist claptrap that periodically engulfed the nation. In this fashion, he became a genuine hero—at least in her eyes. Although she had a dim view of marriage, she had even gone ahead and married him. And now he was sick—maybe dying. "Damn," she said, as tears began rolling down her cheeks. Grabbing a tissue, she wiped her face and blew her nose.

Of course, she was still a feminist. Despite her disappointments, she had nothing against men—just against sexism. In fact, she thought, people weren't evil. They were actually rather beautiful. The real evil lay in institutions that channeled them into harmful behavior.

Sometimes, of course, she wondered where the institutions came from. That was why she had rejected a proposal from some of her women's studies colleagues at UAardvark to work on a new scholarly study, "Gender Segmentation in Southern Mongolian Yurt Production." There were enough studies of sexist and other regressive behavior, she thought. What was really needed now was to develop ways to change it. And that was just what she was going to do!

Feeling a bit better, Ellen stood up, walked to the kitchen, and peered into the refrigerator to see what there was to eat. Not much, it turned out. But that was mostly because she was a vegetarian—and a very strict one, at that. Discovering a bowl of leftover seaweed, she carried it over to the kitchen table and began munching on the green, bitter tendrils. Seaweed, she had to admit, was not exactly comfort food. Even so, anything that tasted like this had to be healthy. And at least it wasn't a dead animal!

To liven up the seaweed a bit, she added a little coconut oil and Himalayan fungus—both of which, she had read, were good for the pancreas. Ellen had never had pancreatic problems. But you never knew if you would have them in the future.

Reverting to her earlier musings, she thought: Yes, people were beautiful in many ways. But it was also easy to be discouraged at times by their apathy in the face of evil. How could they put up with capitalism's rape of the environment? And closer to home, why were UAardvark's faculty and students so passive while this clownish campus administration went ahead building the New Technology Center? Even Jake, despite his wonderful activist background, had a dismayingly burnt-out style and attitude.

At the thought of Jake, though, she couldn't resist smiling again—and wondered idly whether she had looked OK when he stopped by. As a good feminist, she had wrestled for years with her vanity. On the one hand, she knew she was very attractive, with a shapely body and delicate features. Yet, on the other, she didn't want to flaunt them, for she recognized that physical attractiveness had been elevated by sexists into the key attribute of women. So, like many feminists, she had adopted a gender-neutral style of clothing, no makeup, and short hair. But, of course, that didn't prevent her from wanting to look good! She laughed briefly at the contradiction and, then, settled down to drafting her Freedom of Information Act request.

# Chapter 7

## President Dwight Hopkins III

As Ellen pondered the mysteries of human behavior, the nature of evil, and the construction of the New Technology Center, the center's leading proponent, UAardvark President Dwight Hopkins III, was closeted in his office with his miniature racing cars.

"Vroom, vroom," he cried out, moving a tiny car across his broad, polished desk. "There goes Hopkins around the turn, surging to the fore and now—yes, now!—taking the lead. No one can stop him. Vroom, vroom!" Sweat drenched his handsome brow and his eyes took on a mad, glazed look.

Suddenly, the ringing of his office telephone interrupted the drama. Cursing, he picked up the receiver. "What *is* it, Marsha?" he snapped.

"I'm sorry to interrupt you, President Hopkins," his secretary began, "but the dean of humanities, Dr. Huffenpuffer, is on the line and says that it's urgent that he speak with you."

"Damn it, Marsha. Tell him that I'm in a very important conference on academic standards and cannot be disturbed!" With that, Hopkins slammed down the receiver.

Removing his expensive Simonnot Godard handkerchief carefully from his pocket, the campus president wiped his wet, overheated face and began to wonder why the dean had called. Could Huffenpuffer have gotten wind of his plan to close down unnecessary humanities departments like art history, English, foreign languages, and philosophy? He bet those philosophers had never met a payroll—whatever that meant. And what the hell was philosophy, anyway? But, he reasoned, the dean couldn't possibly know of the plan. When it was ready, it would be put forth by Dwight Hopkins alone, and he hadn't discussed it with anyone yet. No, that old fuddy-duddy probably just wanted to talk about hiring someone to teach about the history of the Enlightenment, or some useless crap like that!

President Hopkins—a tall, commanding man of 44 years of age, with a ruddy face and silver hair—was descended from a long line of prominent Americans. They were Virginia slaveholders who, after their rout in the Civil War, had intermarried with the offspring of Yankee business magnates. Hopkins and other family members were proud to recall that their forebears had played key roles in establishing Virginia's racial segregation policies, breaking the Pullman strike, deporting Emma Goldman, and purging subversives from Hollywood, while amassing vast fortunes along the way.

Dwight Hopkins, to be sure, had come from the wastrel branch of the family—a branch that seemed to grow larger as the family grew wealthier. Although his prep school grades and behavior were appalling, he was easily admitted to Yale, thanks to the generations of Hopkinses who had attended that august institution. Indeed, his grandfather, Adolf Hopkins, had even endowed Yale's Institute of Aryan Biology (now tactfully renamed the Bush Life Sciences Institute). Pledging Delta Ipsilon Mu—DIM, the traditional fraternity for men of the Hopkins clan—young Dwight became a great favorite of his fraternity brothers while drinking his way through several years of college. Having failed most of his courses, Hopkins found that even his family connections could not prevent his expulsion from the university. But, after a year abroad on his yacht—where he dried out (somewhat), chased starlets, and acquired a taste for cocaine—his family influence did produce "another chance" at Yale. Here, with much tutoring and some plagiarism, he managed to receive a "gentleman's C" in his courses and to show his leadership abilities by heading up the Young Republican Club (heavily populated by the DIMs).

As a result, Hopkins graduated and then enrolled in an MBA program. But this proved a mistake, for he had reached his limits as a student. After studying hedge fund management for less than two semesters, he dropped out and accepted a job as vice president for development in one of the family firms, WMD Productions, which manufactured triggers for nuclear weapons. Unfortunately, he found this almost as boring as his college courses, especially as he didn't quite know what "development" meant. Over the years, in fact, he spent much of the time simply indulging himself in his hobbies of collecting miniature (and very expensive) racing cars, snorting cocaine, and watching porno videos.

He did keep up his college friendships with the DIMs, however, and these eventually proved useful. Two of his old buddies had been appointed to the board of trustees of UAardvark. And, in the context of higher education's growing reliance on business to sustain itself, good old Dwight—the DIM fraternity bro who could drink anyone under the table— seemed like a first-rate recruit for the university administration. A few phone calls to the other trustees about Hopkins and his corporate connections soon put matters right, and Dwight Hopkins became UAardvark's fifth president.

Hopkins loved the job. Here were all these brainy college professors, the same types who had once given him failing grades in their classes, and he was their boss! What a thrill! Also, of course, he was now able to shape the university to his heart's content—raising tuition to get rid of the lower-class riffraff, eliminating useless programs in which students did nothing but go around reading and thinking, and developing university-business "partnerships." Straightening the sleeves of his Gucci suit and adjusting his designer tie, Hopkins glanced fondly at himself in the ornate mirror that he had ordered installed in his oak-paneled office. "Yes," he thought, "I'm living proof that talent and hard work pay off in modern America."

As the excitement, for the time being, had gone out of playing with his racing cars, Dwight returned them to a desk drawer and locked it with a key. Then, growing restless, he turned on his computer, laboriously typing into the search box: "sadomasochism, sexual fantasies." When the links appeared on the screen, he clicked the first one, his eyes glistening in anticipation. Just as he was examining the possibilities, however, the telephone rang again.

Picking up the receiver, he snarled: "What is it *now*, Marsha?"

"I'm really sorry to interrupt your very important conference, President Hopkins, but your wife is on the line and wants to know when you plan to be home for dinner."

As befit his wealth and social status, Hopkins had married a beautiful, elegant, upper-class woman, Mary Jo Thistlethorpe of Cos Cobb, Connecticut. The Thistlethorpes had made their fortune in the 19<sup>th</sup>-century opium trade, and Mary Jo, as befit their descendants, had emerged from the proper private schools and college as a gracious, attractive wife and hostess. But, after a short period, Hopkins had tired of her, especially her highbrow talk of art and literature. Surely there was something more to life than this. Something a little . . . quirkier.

Returning to his wife's question about the time of his return, Hopkins said, with a deep and weighty sigh: "Tell her I'm not sure about dinner, Marsha. I'm dealing with urgent university business that can't be straitjacketed by artificial time limits. Say that I'll call her back when I'm available."

"Yes sir, I'll tell her," Marsha replied coolly.

Hanging up the receiver, President Hopkins turned again to his computer screen. Carefully reading through the options, he clicked on "whips."

# Chapter 8

## Marsha Skelton

After transmitting the president's message to Mary Jo Hopkins, Marsha put down the phone and snorted in disbelief.

"Does that ignorant, aging frat boy in there really think that anyone believes him?" she wondered. Certainly Marsha didn't. How could she when it was clear enough that, despite his talk of a conference, he was the only person in his office?

Marsha Skelton was a gray-haired, heavyset, 60-year-old African-American woman who had seen UAardvark administrators come and go during her 28-year-long tenure as secretary to the president. If she had not been there to hold things together, the university would long ago have collapsed. She was well aware that she was far brighter, more talented, better organized, and (in the case of Dwight Hopkins) better educated than they were. Having studied at the undergraduate level at Cornell, she had gone on to receive her MA and Ph.D. degrees in physics at the University of Chicago. Had she not been a victim of racial and gender discrimination, she probably would have become a college professor. But now she was a secretary—although a very well-paid one, for her bosses recognized that she was indispensable.

Yes, she mused, she had certainly seen it all on this campus. Shortly after she had arrived at UAardvark, University President Anton Snerdlove had, with great fanfare, launched the Human Psychology Project. Funded by a $17.4 million grant from the I.G. Farben Foundation, the project was designed to determine, through the use of human subjects, the relative attraction of pleasure and pain. Some 200 students volunteered for the experiment, conducted by the UAardvark Psychology Department. Placed in large cages for a four-week period and denied food and drink, the students were free to press a bar and receive a dipper of refreshing fruit juice at any time they pleased. But, when they did that, they would, on random occasions, also receive a painful electric shock. Fairly soon, the students began complaining about these conditions, but— although their complaints were carefully recorded by the team of experimenters—they were kept locked up in their cages and limited to the same painful choices. Only after 12 students had died from malnutrition or shock was the experiment abandoned. Although, for a time, university administrators feared the eruption of a full-scale public scandal, some judiciously-distributed follow-up grants from the foundation kept the story out of the mass media.

Another memorable disaster, Marsha recalled, was generated by President Carol Halfbaked, Snerdlove's successor. Although she was UAardvark's first woman president, Halfbaked—like many old boy administrators—loved to follow football, or at least said she did. As a result, at enormous expense to the university, she arranged for the building of training facilities for the Kokomo Klansmen, Indiana's premier professional football team, on campus. This would provide great financial benefits to UAardvark, she insisted, for admission fees could be charged to the curious, football-mad public, to view the team while training. Plus, she predicted, the state legislature, finally recognizing the value of public education, would start allocating adequate funding to the university. The Klansmen, however, were an unruly lot—even more so than the students. Often bored at night, they would go on drunken binges during which they smashed car windows and sexually assaulted female students. Sometimes they deliberately taunted or otherwise provoked male students, thus giving themselves the opportunity to beat them up. President Halfbaked proved remarkably willing to tolerate this behavior until, one evening, one of the inebriated Klansmen sought to rip off her blouse. In response, she shrieked and slapped him in the face, whereupon he and his buddies proceeded to pick her up and stuff her into a half-filled garbage dumpster. The state legislature was more polite, but failed to come through with any additional funding for the university.

With Halfbaked's departure, Herman Schicklgruber took the helm at UAardvark. Although ostensibly the holder of a graduate degree, President Schicklgruber was a remarkably ignorant individual who spent much of the time in his office doing sit-ups and lifting weights. Like other administrators, though, he had a flair for publicity and, therefore, arranged for the university to give honorary doctoral degrees to all of the Kardashian sisters. Whatever intellectual drawbacks this action had, it did attract a great deal of publicity, not all of it favorable. The following year, at the president's insistence and despite growing protests from the faculty, UAardvark granted an honorary doctorate to Paris Hilton. Meanwhile, overturning departmental decisions, President Schicklgruber denied tenure to numerous young faculty members, two of whom won Nobel prizes in chemistry only a year later.

For a time after the 9/11 attacks and the onset of the "War on Terror," President Schicklgruber seemed in his element. With "Homeland Security" as his watchwords, he instituted frequent police searches of classrooms and dormitories, posted warnings about loose lips sinking ships, arranged for the Pledge of Allegiance to be said before classes, and ordered daily flag drills on campus. But his demand that faculty and students wear uniforms drew open derision and hostility, even from members of these jaded constituencies. To the relief of most of the campus community, Schicklgruber retired in the middle of the academic year to assume a well-paid position as host of a TV reality show. Thereafter, students, faculty, and administrators promptly forgot about their central role in the War on Terror.

Against this backdrop, Dwight Hopkins should have been a relief. He was certainly smoother and less grating than his predecessor. And at least he looked like a university president.

But Marsha couldn't shake the feeling that Hopkins was a dope, and at least as out of place in an institution of higher education as his predecessors had been.

For example, he surrounded himself with administrators who did little except implement bizarre schemes. The latest, organized by the vice president for student motivation, involved posting notices in campus buildings that were designed to create positive images for students. Only that day, the classrooms had been plastered with leaflets proclaiming: "36% of UAardvark Students Remain Sober on Weekday Nights." The fact that this announcement implied that 64 percent of the student body was drunk during the week had not, apparently, occurred to the vice president or to the president.

Also, Hopkins was dishonest. He not only spun dubious yarns about vital conferences, but also hid his fascination with racing cars—yes, Marsha had spotted the ridiculous things on his desk—and dodged work whenever he could. Without her, the university would be in chaos.

Hopkins had a plan, she conceded. But it was an awful one—opening UAardvark to a corporate takeover. Unlike at least some of his predecessors, he had never spoken up and sought to reverse the decline of government funding for the university. Instead, he seemed perfectly happy to turn it into a privately-funded school for rich kids—or at least the rich kids who, like him, were not very bright. As the corporations came through the front door, the intellectual standards of the place were going out the window.

Marsha didn't like that at all. But what could she, a mere secretary—and a member of a thinly-tolerated racial minority group—do about it? She didn't know. For the time being, at least, she would keep her eyes open and her mouth closed. Loose lips, she thought with amusement, could sink ships. But that was not going to happen to *her* ship!

# Chapter 9

## A Meeting at the Pentagon

General Herman ("Buck") Thorkelson of the U.S. Army smiled at his two military colleagues as they took seats in his office: Admiral Thomas ("Skip") Rogers (U.S. Navy) and General Andrew Wilson (U.S. Air Force). Superficially, they were all friends—indeed, comrades in arms. And seated there, they did look rather similar, for they were all big, beefy white men, in their late 50s, with florid faces, crew-cut gray hair, and rows of dazzling medals on their uniforms.

But appearances, General Thorkelson knew, were deceptive. Skip, for example, had a head like a billiard ball, and wore an expensive wig to hide his baldness. Andy had had his uniform redesigned to broaden what seemed to be his shoulders and hide his ever-expanding waist. And when it came to government appropriations, they were intensely competitive. In fact, they were meeting right now to decide how to respond to the latest administration proposal for the military budget, and their smiles were as phony as his.

Andy Wilson broke into his thoughts by saying: "How are they treating you these days, Buck?"

"Not too bad, Andy," he replied. "These pinhead politicians are always trying to cut our most vital military programs, but we're still getting by." By "cut," of course, he meant that the next year's appropriation was reduced from a funding increase of 27 percent to an increase of 24 percent. And that was still pretty good.

Even so, Buck Thorkelson was annoyed. "I was really looking forward to construction beginning on the Complete and Robust Underground Destroyer." Lauded in top corporate and Pentagon circles, the $237 billion high-tech CRUD weapons system was touted as the U.S. answer to the aggressive behavior of Costa Rica.

"Yes," Andy said, "the delay on building CRUD is really a shame. You would think that with the Costa Ricans criticizing Uncle Sammy, those cretins in the White House would wake up and see the danger to U.S. national security." As all three men knew, Costa Rica was the latest military threat to the United States, for its president had questioned the Pentagon's request to conduct nuclear weapons tests on its territory. And, although Costa Rica hadn't maintained armed forces for many decades, this betrayal of the Free World must mean that the tiny nation was up to no good.

At the same time, Buck was canny enough to realize that Andy was probably lying when he commiserated with him over CRUD. Indeed, Andy had almost certainly lobbied against it in hopes of getting a bigger slice of the appropriations pie for the Navy. Buck went on to remark: "It's a damn fine weapons system, and just the thing that, when fired in good ol' Texas, can dig that underground channel right through Mexico and those other greaser nations and explode in the middle of goddamned Costa Rica." Reaching into his desk drawer, he took out a model of CRUD and handed it to the other military officers, who began to play with it on the floor.

"Of course, Buck," said Admiral Skip Rogers, retaking his seat and adjusting his wig, "you must realize that the Sea

Launched Operations Projectile is a much better means of taking out the Costa Ricans."

Buck didn't realize any such thing, and was about to tell his fellow officers just what he thought of the absurd SLOP program when Skip continued: "Also, the Bible clearly shows that God's final judgment upon the unbelievers will come from the heavens!"

Both Buck and Andy, well aware that Skip was a fundamentalist wacko, rolled their eyes at one another. At the same time, though, both men had the sickening feeling that Skip's religious fanaticism might well give him a leg up in their fierce competition to be appointed the new chair of the Joint Chiefs of Staff.

In an apparent attempt to break the gathering tension, Andy asked: "Say, Buck, how does a fella get a cup of coffee around here?" In response, Buck picked up his phone, called his secretary, and ordered coffee for the three of them.

They were all chatting away about the much more agreeable subject of their plans for lucrative, post-government employment with military contractors when Buck's secretary, Sharon Zowee, entered the room with their coffee. Ms. Zowee was an extremely shapely young woman and, as she deposited the tray on Buck's desk, both Andy and Skip stared with fascination at the fullness of her breasts. As a deeply religious individual, Skip blushed while he did it.

Buck, however, concentrated on her feet. Ever since his teenage years, he had been a secret foot fetishist and, at home, maintained a special closet for the shoes of women. On one occasion, his shocked wife had discovered him fondling the shoes. But, as the two of them had little use for one another, that hardly mattered. What did matter was that Ms. Zowee had excellent feet, and for months he had been wondering how he might manage to get a better look at them.

When she left, all three men were sweating.

"Good coffee," Skip mumbled. With images of Ms. Zowee's breasts still fluttering in his brain, he tried to distract himself with thoughts of video games. Skip loved to press the computer buttons and destroy monstrous creatures in explosions. "If only life could be more like that," he mused to himself. "And it would be if I could have SLOP!"

When he managed to refocus on the conversation, Skip found that Buck was talking amiably with Andy about their success in "taking out the ragheads in the Middle East."

"Yes, the gooks gave us a hard time in Indochina," observed Andy, "but we showed everyone what we could do in Iraq and Afghanistan."

Delighted to be back in the territory of the righteous, Skip called out fervently: "Amen!"

With their harmony restored, the three officers agreed that, if the military budget were to remain sacrosanct, it was vital to keep the peace creeps and other subversives on the run by stressing the grave menace of the Costa Ricans to the future survival of the United States.

Indeed, enveloped in good spirits, they even began to swap information on innovations developed by their public relations staffs to burnish their public images. Buck described the new "General Thorkelson's Have a Heart" campaign to provide artificial limbs for children who had lost their arms or legs in war. Skip outlined plans for the "Admiral Thomas Rogers Stay with God" program, which would donate Bibles to prisoners being tortured in Afghanistan. Andy discussed the "General Andrew Wilson Cups for Blind Veterans" drive, which would help the nation's sightless heroes support themselves through more effective street-corner begging.

Suddenly, though, there was a knock on the door and Ms. Zowee entered once again. Skip and Andy looked up eagerly, while Buck looked down. "General Thorkelson, I'm sorry to interrupt," she said, "but there's an important caller on the line for you: Mr. William Swagger V of Corporate Commodities, Incorporated."

"That *is* an important caller," Buck remarked. Turning to Skip and Andy, he said: "Sorry, fellas. I really should take this call. And I think we've accomplished everything we need to. So let's call it a day."

Bounding from their chairs, Skip and Andy shook hands warmly with Buck and, then, headed out of the office. Both wondered if the Army general had lined up a lucrative job with Corporate Commodities, Incorporated.

As soon as the door had closed, Buck picked up his phone. Reverting to the deep, manly voice he employed to charm politicians and corporate officials alike, he purred: "General Thorkelson here."

# Chapter 10

## A Deal with CCInc

William T. Swagger V was sitting in his plush office on the 86th floor of the Corporate Commodities Inc. building in downtown Dallas. While he waited for Buck Thorkelson to get on the phone, he glanced briefly at his casual Brioni suit (recently purchased for $6,077.94) and fiddled with his iPad to check his latest net worth. The amount flashed on the screen: $6.37 billion. That wasn't too bad, he thought. With an entire unit of Corporate Commodities, Inc. (known among business insiders as CCInc) assigned to working 24 hours a day to keep track of his net worth, he checked on it every 10 minutes or so.

Swagger prided himself on being a self-made billionaire. After all, his father had been relatively poor, with only a $117.84 million net worth. And his great-great granddaddy, Billy ("Sugar Cane") Swagger, had started at the bottom. A Louisiana slaveholder, he was almost ruined in the years after the Civil War. Fortunately, though, Sugar Cane was able to draw upon the Ku Klux Klan to clear his county of black farmers, whose land he immediately seized and, later, sold at a handsome profit. Yes, hard work paid off! Sighing deeply, Swagger wished those lazy bastards who worked in his factories, chemical plants, and diamond mines understood that.

His meditation on the virtues of "winners" and the laziness of "losers" was broken by his secretary, who reported that General Thorkelson was on the line.

"Howdy, Buck," he said. "How are they hanging?"

"Why just fine, Bill. How are you and yours?"

The two men chuckled appreciatively at their wit.

Actually, it had taken some time to repair their previously close relationship. Just three years ago, Buck had smoothed the path for the federal government to purchase CCInc's Reliable International Pilotless Overseas Fuel-efficient Fighter (known in the trade as RIPOFF). With 250 planes ordered at $764 million per plane, there was a fat profit to be made on the deal by CCInc. And, of course, it was vital to the national defense, for top military and other government officials viewed RIPOFF as the perfect response to the serious threat posed to the United States by Paraguay. Unfortunately, however, in the first trial run of the supersonic fighter, the wings fell off. And in the second, third, fourth, fifth, and sixth trial runs, the same thing happened, with the planes occasionally crashing into homes, apartment houses, and shopping centers in cities and towns across America. Even after that, Swagger had insisted that, with a little more tinkering, the plane would be in good shape. General Thorkelson, reprimanded by the secretary of defense, was not so sure. As a result, the contract was canceled and CCInc received a mere $87 billion for the work it had done thus far on RIPOFF.

Today, however, Swagger and Thorkelson had another deal on the drawing board, and it seemed more promising.

Getting down to business, Buck asked: "Well, what do you think about moving forward with the plan I suggested? You know I've had a little problem, and, although national security considerations bar my discussing it with you in detail, it does require a solution fairly soon."

Buck's "little problem," Swagger knew from his agents

within the Pentagon, was actually a rather big one. Only about a year ago, in a heated poker game among top U.S. military officers, the stakes had become so high that they had reached the level of military facilities. Buck, the big winner, had come away with a U.S. missile base that was subsequently placed under his command. But the missile base, secretly located in Barren Junction, North Dakota, had proved a constant headache. The soldiers who guarded the nuclear missiles were strung out from the tension and boredom of the work. Frequently they snorted cocaine and popped uppers, downers, and the latest drugs on the market. Sometimes they shot one another. Worst of all, only a week ago, at about three in the morning, one of the more drug-crazed soldiers, viewing his partner as an invader from Mars, had shot him and begun launching two of the missiles. Fearful that nuclear missiles streaking across the sky might trigger a worldwide nuclear war or that they might fall into the hands of enemy nations, the commanding officer on the scene ordered that the missile launch be aborted. And it was, but only by means of blowing up the missiles. The resulting nuclear explosion wiped the missile base off the face of the Earth and left the site plastered with nuclear debris.

Naturally, Buck had covered up this embarrassment as best he could. But, with North Dakotans talking about a strange explosion in the middle of the night and foreign nations reporting heightened levels of radioactivity, he had to act fast to get rid of the nuclear waste before someone discovered it. That was why he had contacted his old friend, Bill Swagger. Maybe CCInc could take care of it quietly and secretly, thus avoiding any possible questions about it from the pinkos in the White House and Congress.

"Buck, I think we have the makings of an agreement here," Swagger observed. "Naturally, I don't know why you suddenly have all this nuclear waste you want removed from that site in North Dakota. But I guess we can handle the job for you. Now, of course, if you want this work kept secret, you can't pay us for it directly. But you could speak to the secretary of defense about the merits of our latest fighter plane—the RIPOFF-2—which we've improved considerably from the earlier model. Yes, there are still a few small problems with the wings. But it does have a very elegant-looking design, which we will be promoting in our new advertising campaign. So how about it?"

Buck was impressed by this very generous offer. All he had to do was to lobby the secretary about RIPOFF-2—not guarantee its purchase. What did he have to lose? "Bill Swagger, you're a good patriot and a good friend. I'll certainly remember that, and the importance of the RIPOFF-2, when I meet with the secretary."

Swagger turned from his iPad (up to $6.38 billion!) and responded graciously: "I do appreciate your confidence, Buck."

Actually, Swagger had a second motive—an even more important one—for removing the nuclear waste. Once it was in the possession of CCInc, he could sell it to other nations for their own use in developing a nuclear capability. And this, in turn, had two benefits. First, CCInc could make a lot of money on such sales. Second, once other nations had acquired a nuclear capability, CCInc could sell the U.S. government new, expensive gadgetry to defend itself from this new nuclear menace.

After exchanging a few further pleasantries, the two men finished up their conversation and rang off. Then Swagger turned his attention briefly to plans for shutting down CCInc's last remaining factories in the United States. They were profitable, he knew, but not nearly as profitable as the corporation's overseas sweatshops, especially those employing children. He smiled as he thought of their nimble little fingers turning out products for CCInc from the Dominican Republic to the Philippines, from Colombia to China. Excited by this state of affairs, he glanced again at his iPad: $6.39 billion!

Even better, his deal with that bozo Thorkelson would reap rich rewards. All he had to do was find a site for the nuclear waste. Pausing for a moment, he thought of just the right place for it. Buzzing his secretary, he said: "Get me Dwight Hopkins on the phone. You know, the president of UAardvark."

# Chapter 11

## Swagger and Hopkins Confer

As the sun's afternoon rays lengthened across his office walls, President Dwight Hopkins held a newly-acquired miniature racing car in his hand and ruminated on the role of a full-size model in his fantasy life. Was sexual bondage possible in the front seat, he wondered? Wouldn't his feet have to be free to step on the accelerator or the brake? But, before this issue could be satisfactorily resolved, the telephone rang.

"What *is* it, Marsha?" he snapped, exasperation evident in his voice.

"Mr. William T. Swagger V is on the line, President Hopkins. Shall I tell him you're in conference?" she asked coyly.

"No, no! Mr. Swagger is a very important person. Put him right through," the president said.

A moment later, a hearty voice bellowed: "Swagger here. How are you, Hopkins?"

"Oh, doing fine, Swagger. And how are things going with your many important enterprises?"

Swagger glanced momentarily at his iPad. $6.41 billion! He chortled: "Very well, very well!"

The two men had first met five years ago at a retreat, held in a luxurious resort on a remote Caribbean island and sponsored by the Club for Greed, an exclusive group of corporate executives who gathered periodically to plan new public policy initiatives. At the time, the Club for Greed was launching the Free All Taxpayers At Last (FATAL) legislation, which would end state taxes on anyone whose income surpassed $1 million a year. Championed in a multimillion-dollar advertising campaign as a surefire job-creator, FATAL had become law in 13 states. Although these states now had the highest unemployment rates in the nation, the club had prepared new legislation to repair this embarrassing glitch. Dubbed Protect Liberty and Guarantee Universal Employment (PLAGUE), the new legislation purportedly would foster increases in U.S. labor productivity and jobs by establishing public flogging of American workers in the nation's factories—at least those factories that still existed in the United States.

Plunging right into what he viewed as the opportunity to court a major corporation, Hopkins said: "I'm delighted that life is treating you well, Swagger. And I'm glad you called. I was just examining the current progress report on the building of the New Technology Center. This is going to be big, really big, Swagger, equipped with the latest technotranstratoparticulate oblattosimulators. Every floor will have its own fluoronanosvibrostomper with its own zelchofigurator. Naturally, I thought that CCInc, as a forward-looking enterprise, should be an investor in this project, which will serve as a model for the superhightech BusEd partnerships of the future."

"Yes, I've been considering that," Swagger replied, pausing briefly to heighten Hopkins's anticipation. "Labor productivity in our Bangladeshi chemical plants has fallen off significantly since the unfortunate explosions in our factories killed 673 workers, burned 1,074, and blinded another 48. And we might even have to pay compensation to the survivors and their families, although we should be able to tie that up in legal knots for at least 30 years. So I've been looking around for a higher return on CCInc's investments, and UAardvark's New Technology Center certainly looks like a good bet along these lines."

"Oh, it is, it is," Hopkins interjected excitedly. "And we're keeping it safe by placing it right in the middle of the campus's new No Demonstrations-No Unions-No Speech Zone. There will also be armed guards at every doorway to maintain security. And the zone itself should be secure from faculty and students, as we have bulldozed all the trees and shrubbery within 50 yards of it and placed electronic sensors around the perimeter. If anyone not carrying the appropriate security badge approaches the center, the sensors will immediately trigger a drone attack upon him—or her!"

"That sounds terrific," Swagger said, "and shows what can be done when a little attention is paid to the needs of business. Anyway, we were thinking of investing about a hundred mil in the center, with a contract granting CCInc sole occupancy of the top floor, where we'd store material from a U.S. government project of ours."

There was a short pause. "What's the material?" asked Hopkins.

"Well, I can't really provide you with much detail," said Swagger, "as this is a top secret venture—one that I have been assured is vital to national security. But let's just call it unsorted nuclear waste, with some quantity of advanced weaponry and human body parts mixed in—a radioactive stew that you wouldn't want for dinner."

The two men chortled.

"No, I guess I wouldn't," Hopkins said, still chuckling. Then, turning more serious, he remarked: "And some of the damned college professors around here probably wouldn't like it, either. But this would all be secret, wouldn't it Swagger? I mean, there's no need to publicize the fact that the center would be storing nuclear waste, is there? There are enough environmentalist kooks and commies around this campus to cause real trouble if word of this got out."

"Of course it would be secret," said Swagger. "In fact, it *must* remain secret for quite a while. The stuff's going to remain in that damn—in that center—for at least a year or two while we locate buyers for it. And, of course, if our sale of the waste is successful, maybe the buyers would be interested in investing in UAardvark's New Technology Center, too!"

"Now that's what I call a win-win arrangement," gushed Hopkins, while Swagger checked his net worth yet again. ($6.40 billion. A decline. Damn those wogs in Bangladesh! No work ethic at all.)

Shaking his head sadly, Swagger wrenched his mind back to Hopkins. "Do you ever get down to Dallas?"

"Every once in a while, when I'm meeting with the big donors from the oil companies."

"Well, sometime you should drop by the Dallas headquarters of CCInc," Swagger said. "Although we're probably going to relocate to Abu Dhabi in about a year, while we're still in Dallas we'd be glad to have you pay us a visit. And, of course, we'd be delighted to take you out for a night on the town. I understand from one of your old fraternity buddies that you were a real hell-raiser back in college."

"Oh, that I was, that I was," recalled Hopkins, his eyes misting over from the memory of it.

"So I'm sure we could have a good ol' time right here in Big D. Drinks, women, maybe a little something to sniff."

"Sounds great," said Hopkins. "I'll be in touch after our lawyers draw up the contract for your company's role in the New Technology Center." Then, after a pause, he added: "You know, I think CCInc and UAardvark are going to have a very profitable relationship!"

"Yes, I think so, too," Swagger said with a smile. "I think so, too."

# Chapter 12

## The Poker Game

That evening, unaware of the partnership shaping up between the university and CCInc, six members of the faculty gathered in the back room of the Galway for their regular poker game, which they held twice every month. They included not only Jake and Harry, but also Helen Meyerson (a tough-talking lesbian from the Political Science Department), Sam Gates (a working-class Marxist from the Economics Department), Gina Sorrentino (a glamorous woman from the Italian Department), and Selwyn Abernathy (an effete monarchist from the Fine Arts Department). Some, like Jake, had been activists in the past and, with the exception of Selwyn, all held liberal or leftwing views. Even Selwyn shared their disdain for the campus administration, and that provided a key factor that drew them together—that and their enjoyment of an occasional night out at the Galway, drinking and playing poker. The stakes were low enough so that no one ever lost or won very much. But they found pleasure in one another's company.

As Sam raked in his winnings from an unusually high-stakes hand, Harry complained, in amusement: "You know, Sam, just because you're an economist, that doesn't mean that you have to win money at poker."

"Well, sometimes stereotypes are true," Sam replied, reaching around his bottle of beer to add carefully to his piles of nickels, dimes, and quarters.

"And sometimes they're not," Gina interjected. "For

example, Dwight Hopkins looks healthy enough—suntanned, trim, and handsome. But every time I see him he makes my skin crawl. I wonder what kind of relationship he has with his wife. Despite her elegant, upper-class style, she seems to have some brains."

"Hopkins does look a little twisted sexually," remarked Helen, "and I don't—of course—mean gay. Even when everyone around here was fawning over Carol Halfbaked, I could see that there was something wrong with her. Only in her case it was a lust for money. Did you know the real reason that she left UAardvark?"

"No," the others murmured.

"She was caught up in a government probe of corporate kickbacks to university administrators. At the time of her departure, government investigators were hot on her trail, and she narrowly escaped them by moving her loot and herself to a remote Caribbean atoll."

"I'm not entirely surprised," Jake said, while examining the cards that Harry had dealt him. Growing a bit tipsy, he glanced over at Gina—a very attractive, passionate older woman with whom he had once had a brief affair. Fortunately for both of them, he thought, by this time the flames of desire had dwindled to sparks—at least in his case.

For a time the friends focused on the mechanics of the game, which Selwyn won easily, having drawn a full house. Pointing to his three kings, he joked: "You see here the power of monarchy!"

The others groaned, while Harry remarked: "You can't really believe in this monarchist rubbish, Selwin."

"Of course I can," Selwyn said. "Naturally, I'd prefer a benevolent monarch—one who was concerned with the welfare of his subjects, one who believed that a healthy peasantry is the backbone of the nation."

"But Selwyn," Harry persisted, "nobody in the United States is a peasant anymore. In fact, almost nobody is a farmer!"

"Well that's the fault of you democrats—overthrowing kings and bringing us the rule of money-grubbing commoners, like that awful Dwight Hopkins." Selwyn paused, then continued: "Just think, if you hadn't made the mistake of revolting against King George III, the United States would be much like Canada today, a country providing national health care for all!" He smiled wickedly while sipping his beer.

Never sure when to take Selwyn seriously, the others laughed while Helen dealt the next hand.

Glancing at his cards, Sam winced and went out, remarking: "We're certainly far from national health care today. Who would ever believe the political program that's now being championed by the Republicans? Restoring the poll tax! Banning all nonmilitary spending! Drafting the unemployed!" He shook his head. "And, unfortunately, the Democrats don't provide much of an alternative. When the Republicans in Congress bring up that scheme for public flogging of workers, the Democratic 'compromise' will probably be to limit the program to businesses with under 100 employees."

"Could be," remarked Gina, who had three jacks showing. When the others quickly dropped out, she raked in her meager winnings. Noticing that no one else was watching, she gave Jake a quick, drunken wink.

Ignoring the provocation, Jake stuck to the theme of gloom and doom, asking: "And what's going on at UAardvark? A complete corporate takeover, lock, stock, and barrel! I wonder why those administration slicksters don't forget about maintaining a university and simply turn it into a local branch of Walmart. After all, we already have corporate advertising everywhere, thousands of consumption-obsessed students, a neutered and compliant workforce, and big parking lots surrounding the campus buildings to accommodate shoppers from the community. What a great shopping center!"

"Careful, Jake, not so loud," Helen said. "The administration might take you up on that."

"Don't worry, that's probably already the plan," Jake retorted.

Harry glanced up from his cards. "Well, maybe it is and maybe it isn't," he said. "But, right now, the cutting edge of the corporate takeover of UAardvark seems to be the New Technology Center. And nobody—at least nobody outside the administration—seems to know what it's going to be used for. Does anyone here have any idea?"

The game halted a minute as everyone thought this over.

"My guess is that it's going to house the latest in torture technology," said Gina, breaking into laughter.

"How about a taser factory?" asked Selwyn. "Police forces everywhere seem to enjoy abusing the citizenry with those kinds of things."

"Actually, I'll bet that the center will be devoted to manufacturing chemical weapons," said Harry. "They never go out of style."

"Or how about a giant mausoleum?" asked Helen. "Maybe it

will serve as the place where rich people are stored after they're iced and preserved for the future. What do you think, Jake?"

Taking his time in answering, Jake said: "Who knows? Around here, reality always seems to outrun imagination. About all I know for sure is that there's not a damned thing we can do about it. Nothing at all." Scowling, he took a long drink of beer.

The others nodded and, looking down at their cards with some discomfort, went back to their game.

# Chapter 13

## In Natasha's Room

As the evening sky darkened over UAardvark, Natasha Randall sat on her bed, with her back against her dorm room wall, toying with a lock of her curly purple hair. One of the advantages of the room was that it was in a corner suite that, relative to the other rooms in Koch Industries Hall, was quite spacious. The major disadvantage was that she had two suite mates, Emily and Ashley. Both, she thought with irritation, were bubbleheads, more concerned with brand-name clothing, makeup, and boyfriends than with anything else.

Natasha also had a boyfriend—or at least a guy who hung around her—named Ray. But he struck her as a jerk and, anyway, she wasn't at all sure she was hetero. Maybe she was lesbian, she mused. Maybe she was bi. She spent a lot of time on this sexual preference question without coming to any definite conclusion. Anyway, she thought, right now she wouldn't mind it at all if Ray just got the hell out of her room and took his iPad—on which he was absorbed in some disgusting video game—with him.

But Ray didn't seem about to leave. Nor did the five other students lying about the larger room in the suite—some on the beds, others on the floor. Drinking beer and smoking pot, they carried on a desultory, often disconnected conversation.

"I said to my parents, like, I have to have that ^#%$# sweater. But they just blew me off," Ashley whined. "The same thing happened when I told them I wanted a new car. &$^(&(^*! My parents totally suck!"

Several of the other students nodded in sympathy and complained about their parents as well. But Johnny, Ashley's boyfriend, continued to focus on doing his 200 sit-ups, his evening quota.

Viewing this as a slight, Ashley called out: "#&#*%%&, Johnny. Didn't you already work out for, like, three hours today over at the gym?"

Scowling, Johnny paused a moment and retorted: "What the ^%(&%$, Ashley. That was with the *%$%*%(* heavy weights. Like, this is for my abs!"

From Ray's video game came an enormous din, as his warlords and warriors clashed in battle.

"Yo Natasha," said Nick, who had had his eye on the attractive young woman for a while. "How'd you manage to answer the question that wacko prof Holland asked the other day in class? You didn't, like, really read that *^%&(^% book, did you?"

"Yeah, I did," she replied. "And it wasn't so bad. You should take a look at it sometime."

"Oh come *on*!" others jeered, while Nick snorted: "We've already got, like, plenty of reading." He held up his iPad. "Look, I've got 47 messages just waiting for me. Like, why am I supposed to read a book too?"

Natasha retorted: "Sometimes books say more than text messages do."

"$*^(*&&%+, Natasha," hollered Emily, adding to her layers of lipstick. "You're too hooked into that old crap. Have you seen the ad for the new Raspberry? It's going to be, like, available next week, and it's really bad. It pays all your bills automatically, sends prerecorded messages to your parents to keep them off your back, and, like—for a small additional fee—arranges to get you all your exam questions two weeks in advance. Oh, yeah, it also, like, picks up 87 TV stations and 174 radio stations and you can set it to record any of their shows. It's the bomb!"

Josh, her boyfriend, put down his beer. "#$%&(^%, that's awesome. You mean I can see any &^)*%(%(^ night's show of *How Much Meat Can You Eat?* that I want? Wow! That's, like, the greatest reality show in the world."

"Hey dudes," said Johnny, having finished his sit-ups and started on bicep-building curls with his dumbbells. "What do you think about trying out for the Pitbulls? That outfit is totally cool."

"(^%(&)%$#@," Nick said. "I'm not sure I got the time for it." Nick was the pledgemaster for the campus chapter of the Sigma Omega Theta (SOT) fraternity, and he was busy making life as miserable as possible for that year's pledges—a number of whom had dropped out after a bad reaction to that fraternity's hazing procedures, including extensive water-boarding. "Plus," Nick explained, "me and the other SOTs are gonna, like, start a big campaign to restore UAardvark to the rank it had two years ago as America's number one party school."

"Man, that's super awesome," Josh conceded, taking another swig of beer. "We never shoulda lost that title. Parties are so much better than all these damned classes!"

"When did you ever go to classes, Josh?" asked Phil, a tall, bespectacled, thoughtful type who secretly enjoyed the courses—or at least most of the courses—he was taking. "I always see you hanging around the video game rooms or the gym."

"Oh, I attend every now and then," Josh replied. "If I don't show up occasionally, like, I forget what (*&^(^%&^% course I'm taking."

Most of the others laughed appreciatively.

"But they're so boring," Josh continued. "They're just mad boring! Things are much more exciting on the outside. Like, you never know what the @$*&^% buildings on campus are going to be renamed. Or what's going to happen around here tomorrow."

"Yeah," Natasha said, suddenly perking up. "What do you think that new construction site is for—the one with the armed guards around it?"

"*&^)*^)%)&#. Who knows?" Nick answered with a shrug. "Whatever."

"I heard it's going to be called the New Technology Center," Phil said. "With those creepy suits running this place, that could mean anything." Then, glancing over at Natasha, a girl he found very interesting—and very alluring in an offbeat way—he added: "It would be great to find out some more about it."

But no one, not even Natasha, followed up. Meanwhile, Ray continued to play his video game. The clang of swords on shields echoed through the room.

Natasha glanced over at the Practice Smart Sex poster on her bedroom wall. Having swiped it from the cafeteria, she had used a magic marker to alter it—drawing a giant condom around a picture of campus officials—and taped it above her desk. But no one seemed to notice it—except maybe Phil, who she now remembered had smiled when he saw it.

Suddenly, Emily blurted out: "^%(^)&(*!"

"What's the matter, Emily?" asked Ashley.

"I swallowed my &)*(%&*%$ bubblegum, that's what," she said. "I forgot, like, it was in my mouth when I drank my beer."

Everyone laughed, except Natasha and Phil. Looking around, Natasha decided she had had enough, and wanted to get out of there. Grabbing her jacket, she headed for the door.

"Where are you going, Natasha?" the others called out.

"To the library," she said, adding the barb: "Hey, you remember that building, don't you?"

"Oh $%$&^%(, Natasha," Josh said. "Lighten up. Like, we're having a party."

Halting at the door, she paused and, then, returned reluctantly to her seat on the bed. But she thought to herself: "Looks more like a funeral to me!"

# Chapter 14

## United UAardvark Faculty

The atmosphere was not much more inspiring at the executive committee meeting of UAardvark's faculty union, held the following day in the Ace Athletic Supporter Room of the campus United Brands Building.

The United UAardvark Faculty (UUF) had been fairly somnolent since its founding at the birth of the university. Although UUF went through the motions of meetings and other sedate activities, "Solidarity Forever"—sung at its campus-wide gatherings—now meant little more to most of its leaders than solidarity among themselves. Few faculty members attended UUF's activities or identified with it, even as the university slid down the slippery slope toward corporatization. Nevertheless, most UUF leaders, amid their union-funded eating and drinking junkets, managed to convince themselves that they were doing an excellent job.

The top leaders had been at the helm of the union for ages. The UUF president, Wilma Welsh, had served as union executive committee member, vice president, and president for a total of 19 years. Although she had once looked fairly conventional, in recent years she had grown gaunt and had been turning an oddly green color. Together with the black clothing she now wore and her prickly temperament, these features led her, on occasion, to be referred to, privately, as "The Witch."

The current vice president, Igor Cheney (better known as "The Chihuahua" thanks to his resemblance to a small, yapping dog), had occupied these posts as well, and prided himself on having served in the union leadership for 34 years. The Chihuahua, like The Witch, had a very undistinguished academic career. Originally hired to teach about his specialty, the dung beetle, he had obtained tenure in the Biology Department at a time when scholarship was viewed as unnecessary. As both Wilma and Igor had accomplished little of a professional nature, they secured their major importance in their union posts—posts to which they had been elected in what were usually one-candidate races.

The rest of the union executive committee was a mixed bag. Other opportunists and time-servers could also be found in the UUF leadership ranks, where The Witch seemed to have them under her spell. But, in recent years, as conditions on the campus deteriorated, more activist-oriented individuals had been elected to the executive committee, including Jake, Gina, and Sam, who could not quite abandon the notion that a union had a role to play in defending workers' rights. As a result, to the dismay of Wilma and Igor, their longtime control of union matters was beginning to slip from their grasp.

Wilma led off the meeting—a luncheon gathering in which executive committee members chomped leisurely on the catered meal—with her President's Report, a sort of statement from the throne that lasted about an hour. It included lengthy descriptions of her latest vacation and of the wonderful dinners she had eaten. (Jake wondered what these dinners could have been, as the only thing she seemed to consume at union luncheons was a strange, green, bubbling concoction—perhaps, he thought, the source of her odd complexion.) Excited by the subject,

Igor piped up to comment on various hotels he had roomed at during out-of-state conventions. Then Wilma resumed her report, remarking on how much she had needed the vacation, given how hard she was working for the union. At this juncture, several of her enchanted followers spoke up to compliment her on her hard work and—although it remained unclear just what this work was—they led the gathering in applauding her. Jake, like some of the others present, had visions of her on vacation in a Transylvanian castle, with bats flitting about.

Wilma now turned to complimenting her favorites. Muriel, it seemed, had been in a fund-raising race for the American Cat Lovers Society. Bill had been written up in the *Aardvark Enterprise* for the attractive condition of his lawn. Harriet had appeared in an amateur theatrical performance of *Nunsense*. Applause again followed dutifully.

Things got a little hotter, though, when Wilma, between hefty gulps of her drink, reported on a recent campus-wide meeting that she had addressed alongside President Hopkins on the subject of the university's future. "Dwight was magnificent," she gushed, using her napkin to wipe away a blob of green slime on her chin. "And he announced that he is arranging to have a statue of me erected in honor of my campus leadership. That's a great honor for the union!"

Gina now interrupted. "Oh come on, Wilma. Hopkins spent most of the time lauding the administration. He also sneered at UUF, saying unions created unnecessary conflict on the campus."

"Yes," said Sam. "I was there, too, and I certainly came away with the impression that he had nothing but scorn for our union and any other."

Turning her withered neck slowly and glaring at Sam, The Witch retorted: "That's a completely false interpretation of what Dwight said. From my many meetings with him, I can assure everyone that he always has union and faculty interests at heart. I certainly hope you haven't spoken to anyone else about the campus meeting in that fashion. It could be really dangerous—for you," she said sharply, "and for everyone else."

"You're right as always, Wilma," yelped The Chihuahua. "That kind of negative talk is only going to provoke the administration to limit the many privileges we already enjoy on this campus."

Although some members of the executive committee nodded vigorously in approval, others rolled their eyes at what they considered one more sign of their officers' coziness with campus management.

Gina, however, was not willing to let it go. "The administration is exactly what is undermining our working conditions and security on this campus. It has no respect for education, and has implied that it feels free to 'reorganize' the university whenever it feels that would help it rake in additional corporate cash."

"I can't deal with this kind of talk," snarled The Witch, who sprang to her feet and stormed out the door. Looking at one another in astonishment, the rest of the executive committee members, cut adrift, chatted among themselves until, 10 minutes later, Wilma returned with a new pitcher of her green, viscous drink, calmer now and acting as if nothing had happened.

Sam, however, raised another issue—that of the campus cleaning and maintenance workers—who had been working without a contract for the past 23 months. Although they belonged to a different union, he noted, their wages were pitiful and their working conditions abysmal. Thus UUF should come to their aid. He proposed a financial contribution of $50 to assist them in printing leaflets about their plight.

With The Witch busy chugging her bubbling brew, her usual supporters substituted for her by sounding the alarm.

"What do we really know about these people?" one of them said.

"Don't we have enough problems of our own?" asked another.

"That kind of action might cause us legal difficulties," said a third.

Setting down her glass sharply, The Witch joined the attack. "Sam, you and other troublemakers"—and here she glanced at Gina and Jake—"are always causing difficulties. The administration would give me a lot of grief about any collaboration with that other union. Plus, any financial assistance to it would undermine our ability to use that same money to cover our own vital expenses."

Recognizing that he lacked the votes to carry the issue, Sam dropped it in disgust.

The officers and their allies sighed in relief and turned to more important matters. "Angela," said The Witch, "I think you had an item of business to propose."

"Yes," said Angela. "I've been investigating UUF's possible purchase of 2,000 pairs of pink, heart-shaped sunglasses, with the statement 'I Love UAardvark' printed on them. These would be wonderful items to distribute to our members, and would remind them of the vital role played by our union. As we'd be buying them in bulk—and as they would be partially subsidized by the Dow Chemical Company, whose logo would appear on both lenses—they would cost us only $12,346.78 plus tax."

"That's a great idea," said another executive committee member. "Maybe we should order 3,000 pairs of them!"

To Jake, who for some time had wondered why he participated in such meetings, it seemed that the ensuing discussion of sunglasses continued endlessly. After about 25 minutes of it, he left the room in search of some fresh air.

# Chapter 15

## Wilma

Following the union meeting, Wilma headed home in her old, rattletrap Cadillac. She could easily have afforded a better, more modern car. But this clunker had the features that she coveted: a dull black color, a powerful motor, and pointy tail fins. A sleek Batmobile was sinister, even creepy—just what she wanted.

Wilma had learned some time ago from her spies within the union that her critics referred to her derisively as "The Witch." Well, she could take it. In fact, she loved it!

And why shouldn't she? Yes, years back, Wilma had begun her academic career as the very model of a bouncy, pony-tailed cheerleader. Never particularly bright or attractive, she nevertheless had enough savvy to recognize that that conventional, inoffensive style was probably sufficient to pull her through to tenure. And, combined with a certain low cunning, it did.

But she soon realized that playing the role of a dimwitted bimbo was not how real power was secured, exercised, and maintained. Studying power as she had never bothered studying her professional field of bovine nutrition, she gradually shed her old persona for one that could inspire fear and obedience. For a time, she looked to the examples of Mussolini and Stalin for guidance. Not overly scrupulous, they had risen from humble circumstances to supreme power, crushing their critics along the way. But, although that had considerable appeal to Wilma, she was not sure how she was going to replicate their admirable success, particularly in the more humdrum conditions of American life. Also, they seemed to have gotten a bum rap from the historians, the bleeding-heart liberals, and other subversives.

Fortunately, at this point, when Wilma might have grown discouraged, she had discovered witches. No, not actual witches, but the witches of fairy tales and other fiction. Here, she thought, were some really tough, hard-boiled women who weren't troubled by petty scruples! And they looked fearsome, too—much more terrifying than smiling Uncle Joe Stalin.

Suddenly, Wilma's reminiscences of the past were interrupted by the opportunity to pass a slower-moving car. Gunning her motor and roaring past the offending vehicle, she screamed at the driver: "Get off the road, you slow-ass *^)^%$)#^!"

Settling back into her reverie after this diversion, Wilma again recalled fondly the new appreciation she had gained of witches. Yes, they were cruel, merciless, and sometimes sexy— in a strange, violent sort of way.

Naturally, she had joined Aardvark's local coven. But, alas, that was a mistake. What a namby-pamby group! They were certainly weird and unconventional enough. And yet they insisted that they were perfectly harmless, loving types. Throughout history, they said, witches had been persecuted and misunderstood. All they wanted to do was to help people! "$%(^*&)$#@," Wilma muttered. "What kind of a life is that? I might as well become a social worker!" So, with some regret, she quit the coven and turned back to the wicked witch model in fiction, which was much more appealing.

As the stoplight turned green, Wilma noticed that an elderly woman was still hobbling across the street with the aid of a cane. Smiling, she stepped on the Cadillac's accelerator and shot forward, mumbling that she would "give that old %(^($#^$ a good scare." The woman, though, proved less flappable than Wilma had hoped, and even gave her the finger. Wilma hissed at her in return.

Fairly soon, though, Wilma's thoughts reverted to the measures taken in her successful career.

While gradually carving out her new life as a witch, Wilma had begun to see the campus union as a road to power. With minimal academic qualifications, she didn't seem likely to attain much influence in her department or in her field. But, through the union, she had the opportunity to meet with management, where the real campus power resided. Of course, opposing the administration would have been counterproductive, provoking the wrath of campus management. But supporting it . . . well, that was another matter. It certainly added to her influence and power.

In her role as union president, she had never had any understanding of or desire to employ the class struggle rhetoric spouted on occasion by union hotheads. She wasn't interested in challenging the boss. She wanted to *be* the boss! Naturally, when among union activists, she didn't mention this fact. Instead, she dispensed favors to union members, much as an old-style ward politician once distributed turkeys to his constituents on Thanksgiving. And she still showered praise and favors on those who followed her lead. By contrast, she responded with a strong dose of hostility and derision to members and leaders who dared to cross her—most of whom fell away from the union in disgust.

The Chihuahua (yes, she had learned of his nickname, too, and was even amused by it) had facilitated her rise to power within United UAardvark Faculty. Old Igor, of course, was excited by younger, dominating women, and she knew it. On some level, she was even grateful for his assistance. But those days as a novice were well in the past. Now she had bigger fish to fry.

Meanwhile, she would have to work on smashing the challenge from Gina, Sam, and Jake, who were encouraging a spirit of resistance that might endanger her plans for the future. Well, she'd see what she could do to intimidate them.

Wilma uttered a cackle and decided that it was not quite right. Before unleashing it in public, she would have to give it some additional practice.

# Chapter 16

## Hells Angels

As Jake hurried down the steps of the United Brands Building, he decided to stop by his office in the Walmart Building to pick up his mail before continuing on to an English Department meeting. After swinging by the department mail room, he headed for his office with the intention of leafing through the assorted advertisements and administration notices before the meeting began.

When he arrived there, three massive, hulking men were standing outside his door, filling much of the hallway. The men, ranging between 200 and 300 pounds each, sported shaved heads (one with a pigtail), black leather jackets adorned with spikes and chains, massive, muscular arms covered with tattoos, muscle shirts, dirty jeans, and heavy black boots. Students and faculty passing them in the hall kept their distance. But Jake was glad to see them, for they had all been students of his about three years ago in the poetry course he used to teach at the Aardvark maximum security prison.

"Sal, Frankie, Crusher—how are things going?" he asked, slapping them on their broad backs.

"Pretty good," said The Crusher, with a grin that exposed significant gaps in his teeth. One of his ears was also missing a few pieces. Formerly Mikos Partsopolis, The Crusher was the largest of the group, a Hells Angel, and a ferocious street fighter. He had been jumped two years before by five members of the Terminators, a rival gang, and had suffered some injuries—fewer, though, than his assailants, who had had to be hospitalized. Some, in fact, still were. Now, smiling at Jake, he asked: "Would it be OK if we come in and toss some ^)^%)$#%@ around?"

"Sure," said Jake. "That sounds good."

When they were all seated in his office, Big Frankie (Franklin Moorhead)—his broad chest encased in a jacket emblazoned with "Stomp Them Right and They Won't Bother You Again"— began by explaining that all of them had really enjoyed Jake's course. "Yeah," he said, "we liked that &_(%*&# poetry so much that we reorganized our motorcycle gang, the Kickass Avengers, into a cool-ass poetry study group."

"That's right," said Sal the Bear (Salvatore DiGiovanni), unable to contain his excitement any longer. "We got the Daffodil Poetry Club up and runnin' now, and we been readin' that #*&%)^)(*&^ 16th-century poetry. Then we use that ^) (%@*# to analyze our own personal aesthetic dimensions. You know, the Terminators don't know half the $(^(&^%$%—the literary canon—that we do. And right now, we're deep into &^%*&^)*# feminist poetry."

The Crusher nodded happily, while Big Frankie cracked his knuckles in approval.

"But what's all this corporate (%(*&^)^$% doin' aroun' here?" Sal asked. "This place looks like a *^)^%^*) McDonald's!"

Jake laughed. "Well, the big boss of this place—the university president—likes to maintain a 'business-friendly' environment. Don't you like it?" he asked, provocatively.

"It makes we want to puke," said Frankie. "All them great ideas reduced to sellin' $*%^(*)(&^%." With that, he spat into Jake's wastebasket.

Jake laughed again. "Seriously, I couldn't agree with you more. It's a real disgrace."

Everyone nodded.

"But, anyway," said Jake, "why'd you stop by today?"

"Well, we could use your help with a coupla literary issues," explained The Crusher, adjusting his chains as he leaned his great bulk forward. "We been readin' Christopher Marlowe's 'The Passionate Shepherd to His Love,' which is ^)&*% good. And then we figgered it was only fair to read Sir Walter Raleigh's 'The Nymph's Reply to the Shepherd.' So we did. And it was real discouragin'! What a %*&^)(*& that guy Raleigh musta been. Anyway, we didn't unnerstan' what Raleigh meant when he wrote: 'Philomel becometh dumb.'"

"Oh, I can explain that," said Jake. "In Greek legend, Philomela was a maiden with a slit tongue. She was later turned into a nightingale."

"Well, that ain't so great," remarked Sal. "Just one more ^%(%*%)%$ putdown from that %$(&%(^, Raleigh."

"I think you guys are just romantics," said Jake, smiling.

Sal, Frankie, and The Crusher paused to give that some thought, but then turned to the second thing on their minds.

"And here's an interpretive issue," said The Crusher. "In the 43rd sonnet of Elizabeth Barrett Browning's *Sonnets from the Portuguese*, she writes of 'the ends of bein' and ideal Grace.'" Now I been thinking that 'ideal Grace' must refer to the grace o' God, right? But what do you think Browning was gettin' at when she wrote about 'the ends of bein'? It's got the Daffodils into a real heated literary debate."

"Yeah," said Frankie. "It got so bad that Crazy Ernie rabbit-punched me in the gut, and I smashed him over his &#$*%(&^ head with the beer pitcher."

When Jake suggested that they try to avoid violence in their literary disputes, Sal—hurt by this suggestion—asked: "Well, ain't this %$%(^*&# important?"

"Yes, it is," admitted Jake. "But, in literary circles, we only attack one another with words. You know—bad reviews in journals, critical commentaries at convention panels, and malicious gossip."

"I think I'd rather be (^%^*(&$ rabbit-punched," said Sal, and they all laughed at that.

"Anyway," Jake said, getting back to Browning, "my guess is that she meant 'the ultimate.' Or maybe 'infinity.'"

"That's what I thought," The Crusher replied, as tears sprang into his eyes. "You know, I'm a pretty sensitive guy, and that phrase 'the ends of bein'' reaches me, down deep, down %(^*&^) deep. I been writin' my own poetry on a similar theme." His tears now turned to sobs.

As Sal and Frankie moved over to hold the sobbing Crusher, thereby forming a mass of about 800 pounds of muscle and fat, Sal said, soothingly: "That's all right, Crusher, let it out, let it all out." Then, turning to Jake, Sal explained: "Recently he's been gettin' in touch with his &^%^&%# inner child."

Jake nodded sympathetically. Then, noticing the time, he said: "Look, guys, I gotta go to a department meeting right now. But feel free to stay here and work this through. I'll be back in about an hour, OK?"

The three Hells Angels, all now crying and hugging one another, waved as Jake went out the door. He figured that, although they weren't students, if anyone complained about their presence in his office, the campus security guards would be too frightened to try to remove them.

# Chapter 17

## The English Department

Heading down the hall, Jake entered a large conference room where most members of the English Department were already assembled.

It was a remarkably diverse and contentious group. Some were anarchists, one was an ivory tower Marxist-Leninist, and several were out-and-out fascists, Republicans, or both. Many were simply apolitical. Their specialties ranged widely, including homoerotic themes in *The Book of Job*, premonitions of the Internet in the works of Ben Jonson, and 13th-century Macedonian fiction. Jake was particularly intrigued by the claim of one of his colleagues that she was an expert on the literary works of Sylvia Buttonhook—a figure who probably didn't exist but could not be proved fictitious without members of the department being willing (as they were not) to admit that they had never heard of her.

Not everyone was present—especially department members who were feuding with the dominant faction. A portion of the English Department had been trying for years to secede and establish a new Department of Harlequin Romances. But, as the two leading proponents of the secession plan hated one another, they never managed to meet and agree on a strategy for implementing it. Frightened at the prospect of seeing one another, they usually avoided attending department meetings.

Despite the undoubted intelligence of English Department

members, Jake knew that this meeting would provide another exercise in futility. People outside of academia might think that, when professors of English gathered together, they discussed literature or related subjects. But insiders knew that this was far from the case. In department meetings, they never discussed literature or anything akin to it. Even when department members were persuaded to make a presentation to their colleagues on their own research, almost no one bothered to attend. The sad fact was that department meetings were invariably devoted to trivia.

As Jake sat, waiting for the meeting to begin, he thought of the many things his colleagues could—and probably should— be discussing. These included the terrible cutbacks in public funding for the university, the rapidly-rising tuition that was effectively ending educational opportunity for many students, the corporatization of UAardvark, the mysterious mission of the New Technology Center, the declining caliber of the student body, and the growing disinterest among faculty in teaching and among students in learning. These things, however, were all considered givens—located beyond political walls that could not be breached. Discussion would be confined within their narrow parameters, which meant that trivia would prevail.

Even things that were clearly the traditional prerogative of the faculty—such as grading students—had been slipping from their hands without resistance. The administration not only undermined the credibility of the grading system by promoting student evaluations of faculty, but also didn't hesitate to alter grades when students or their parents complained about them. Under the surface, faculty members were irritated by these encroachments on their turf. But they did not use department meetings to discuss them.

About the only time department members felt a sense of power was when they met to vote on tenure and promotion cases. Then they had their knives out, at least figuratively, for those of their colleagues whose personalities or political stances annoyed them. But, with the administration increasingly ignoring faculty recommendations in personnel cases, much of the excitement had gone out of these meetings, as well.

As a few more department members entered the room, looking anxious (if untenured) or bored (if tenured), Jake chatted with a couple of old friends near him. None had much idea of what the meeting would cover, or felt that it would deal with anything of consequence.

Finally, when it appeared that maximum attendance had been secured, the department chair, Jeremiah Wigglethorpe, rapped his knuckles on the conference table to get everyone's attention. Wigglethorpe was a literary theorist of the Foucaultian type. Students found him totally incomprehensible but were happy enough to take his courses, for he slept through most of his classes, as they did, too. At the moment, though, he was sufficiently awake to get the meeting going.

Clearing his throat, Wigglethorpe began: "Welcome to the final English Department meeting of the semester. I am sorry to report that there are currently lawsuits against this department or its members for harassment, sexual exposure, criminal negligence, absence from classes, and inadequate education. We will certainly turn to these matters in due course."

"That means never," Jake whispered to a faculty member sitting next to him.

"But, first," said Wigglethorpe, "let us take up a matter that I know is troubling all of us: the allocation of space in the department refrigerator."

Tuning out, Jake imagined feature films being screened on the inside of his eyelids for the next 13 minutes. Then he returned his concentration to the discussion just as department members began grappling with another weighty issue: registration procedures and registration forms—of which there were a great many—for the fall semester. Within a minute, growing weary of the discussion, he tuned out again.

After another 19 minutes, Jake forced himself back to consciousness. He noticed, with some degree of self-righteousness, that at least half his colleagues seemed to be dozing in place. A number had their eyes open. This was a good trick if you could manage it, he thought, but their snoring belied their wakefulness. The discussion, however, ground on, and now seemed to be focused on the appropriate deadline for declaring a double major—as good a subject as any, Jake concluded, for another time out.

Some 27 minutes later, Jake awoke with a start. Wigglethorpe still sat in his chair, but was now clearly dozing, as were all the other faculty members remaining in the room. The silence was soothing, Jake admitted to himself, and he could better understand why students liked Wigglethorpe's courses.

Even so, he had other things to do, including checking in on what his literary tyros from the Hells Angels' Daffodil Poetry Club were doing in his office. He wondered particularly what

The Crusher's poetry was like. Did this behemoth use iambic pentameter or a more modern form? At the least, Jake hoped the trio in his office had been able to pull themselves together without smashing any of the furniture or terrifying the security guards. Poetry certainly was powerful stuff!

Careful not to disturb anyone's slumbers, he quietly arose from his seat and, with a grin, tiptoed out of the room.

# Chapter 18

# The Cleaning and Maintenance Workers

In sharp contrast to most members of the English Department, the campus cleaning and maintenance workers were not reluctant to discuss what was going on at UAardvark, both in concrete terms and more abstractly.

That very same evening, 11 of them—eight men and three women—sat on folding chairs, arranged in a circle, in the corner of the main boiler room. The boiler room was located off "the Tunnels," a vast work space under the campus buildings that was usually filled with steam, smoke, and noxious fumes. Having put in the first five hours of their shift, they were taking their break while meeting, secretly, for the third session of their self-taught course, Marx's Contribution to Working-Class Liberation.

"Well," said Tom Rowley, the young, black Jamaican immigrant who chaired the gathering, "has everyone been reading the assigned selections by Karl Marx?"

"Of course," some muttered. Others tapped their books and waited impatiently.

"It was easier to get hold of a copy of *Das Kapital* than I thought," said Eva, a middle-aged white woman with a furrowed brow and gold-rimmed glasses. "I found it on the bookshelf of that economics teacher, Sam Gates. Cleaning up his office at night gave me a good chance to read it."

"That's how I got to discover Trotsky's *History of the Russian Revolution*—I read it in Professor Anderson's office," said Juan, a recent immigrant from Mexico. "You can get a pretty good education at this place, at least if you look around the faculty offices."

Andy, a blue-eyed mountain boy from Kentucky, interrupted, chortling: "But there's nothing worth looking at in the offices of the administrators—except maybe the porn magazines!"

Everyone got a laugh out of that.

Determined to steer the discussion back on track, Tom asked them what they thought of Marx's analysis.

"Man, he certainly beats around the bush," Andy said. "It took me a long time to figure out that all he's getting at is that the bosses screw the workers. Why not just come out and say it without writing all that stuff?"

"Maybe he needed to publish to keep his teaching job," suggested Eva, tongue in cheek.

Tom broke into a grin. "No, he wasn't a college teacher. And Marx didn't have a regular job by the time he wrote *Kapital*." He paused, and then threw out another question: "Do you think *Kapital* bears out Erich Fromm's ideas about Marxist humanism?"

"Not really," said Jaime, a refugee from El Salvador. "By the time Marx wrote *Kapital*, he seems to have abandoned humanism for a more economic model. And that's not a bad thing. At least he keeps the focus on what the capitalist bloodsuckers do to the workers."

Heads nodded in approval.

Unlike the students at UAardvark, the cleaning and maintenance workers were voracious readers and, for the most part, were quite class conscious. Nor was this totally surprising, for many were immigrant workers, and came from countries where they had a far better education than most Americans received from their television programs. Also, they put in 10-hour workdays, six days a week, for a pittance, and dangerous accidents in the Tunnels were frequent.

They did have a union, and would have gone on strike long ago if strikes among public sector workers had not been prohibited by state law. Moreover, they realized that, if they were to go out on strike, they would need defenders on the campus against what they knew would be management ruthlessness and state government repression. But they didn't see any sign of allies. So, with the scales heavily weighted against them, they felt that all they could do at present was to read leftwing classics (secretly, of course) and keep an eye on the "objective situation"—a situation that, given the administration's commitment to corporate priorities, did not look at all promising.

"All right, let's get down to earth here," Tom said. "Do you think that Marx's picture of 19th-century bosses exploiting workers still holds up today?" An explosion of anger and cursing erupted from the assemblage.

"Of course, it does!" shouted one worker.

"Our bosses are %#@$)()& bastards!" stormed another.

"Jesus, which side are you on, man?" grumbled yet another. Someone tossed a roll of paper towels at Tom.

"OK, OK," said Tom, laughing. "I was just trying to get a discussion going!"

"You know, I've been reading their memos—the ones those vice presidents and the other administrators have in their computer files," Maria said, "and they have a lot of contempt for us. These guys are just 21$^{st}$-century Social Darwinists."

"How'd you get to see their memos?" asked Peter, a somewhat more conservative, skeptical worker, maybe even a closet Republican—although the others hoped not.

"Well, when you live in the vice presidents' offices, you get lots of opportunity to go through their computer files," she said. Maria and her family had taken advantage of the fact that most administrators spent only one or two days a week in their offices. With that in mind, they had worked out a plan that enabled them to move from office to office without ever encountering the official occupants. Increasing numbers of other workers, attracted by the prospect of free housing, were doing so as well.

"Sometimes," Maria added, "I just can't stand the ignorance of those guys. So I go through their memos and correct the spelling and grammar. But I guess it doesn't make any difference. No one reads them, anyway."

"I'm not in their offices full time, like some of you are," Andy said. "But sometimes I find useful things in them. So I bring home an extra chair or file cabinet for my family."

"Yeah, man!" someone hollered. "That's the way!"

Andy grinned. "After all, 'property is theft.' At least that's what an anarchist writer, a French dude named Proudhon, said in a book that I found on Professor Sorrentino's bookshelves."

Eva decided not to let that go. "You know, the Marxists and the anarchists came to a parting of the ways in the late 19$^{th}$ century, and the Marxists had a much better case."

This inspired a heated argument among those present, with Tom serving as the referee.

Just then, however, the boiler room door creaked open and Stan Slobodov, their supervisor, entered the room. "What's going on here?" he asked, suspiciously.

"Stan, what a pleasure to see you," said Tom, in a tone that clearly didn't match his words of welcome. "We were just using our break to talk about the shocking nudity in these new Hollywood films. Isn't it terrible?"

"Yeah," said Slobodov, "a good Christian can't hardly take his kids to a movie any more without seein' naked bodies, and lesbians, and worse." Slobodov was a staunch fundamentalist, and often rambled on for hours about the Bible, sin, and the devil. But tonight he was in a hurry, and merely said: "Time to get back on the job! There's lotsa chemicals in the Tunnels that's gotta be mopped up, and also lotsa classrooms that's gotta be cleaned yet."

"@^%$#& slavedriver," a few of the workers muttered among themselves in Spanish as they rose to their feet. Another mouthed: "Tool of the bosses."

Not quite sure what they were saying, Slobodov nevertheless gave them a nasty glare.

"There are a lot of faculty offices that need cleaning up," Eva said politely, with a wink at the others. "Those professors are always leaving their books lying around. It really slows us down," she added, with a smile.

"I'll get the administration to send them a memo about that," Slobodov said, scowling and scribbling something, with difficulty, in his notebook. "What good are their damn books, anyway?"

# Chapter 19

# The Christian Patriots

Few of the maintenance workers would have been surprised to learn that Slobodov was a member of the Christian Patriots, a semi-secret Christian Nationalist organization that was meeting that weekend for its monthly training camp.

Here, at the Americanism Defense Fortress, a broken-down farm outside of town, two dozen Patriots gathered in their camouflage uniforms, amid fluttering American and Confederate flags, and honed their martial skills through target practice, hunting, and war games. Not all of this was easy for the Patriots. As a group of men mostly in their 40s and 50s, they had grown porcine, with large, sagging bellies, and they found it difficult to crawl across the muddy, rocky ground while dodging machine gun fire. In fact, only last year, two of them had been badly wounded, while another three had pulled their backs, causing them to be laid up for weeks. Although the Patriots were supposed to be bivouacking in tents, most now slept in campers or small trailers, some of them air conditioned.

Despite the difficulties, though, the weekend training camps were generally quite pleasant. The men found getting away from their wives and children very enjoyable, and they certainly didn't miss sweating over the home improvements that they had been promising for months. Also, it was fun to be given military ranks and to go around saluting one another—practicing for the day when the nation, thrown into turmoil by the liberals and the colored, would have to be defended by gun-wielding, patriotic Christian Americans. Best of all, though, they enjoyed sitting around a roaring campfire at night, reaching into their cooler chests, pulling out sandwiches and cold bottles of beer, and discussing how the greatest of all nations should handle the terrible threats that confronted it: the liberals, the secular humanists, the Muslims, the illegal (and legal) immigrants, multiculturalism, the intellectuals, gun control, the colored, women's lib, abortionists, subversive books, the ACLU, and sex education in the public schools.

The Christian Patriots used to be a chapter of the Aryan Nations and, before that, the Ku Klux Klan. But, in recent years, they had reorganized and, with the change of name, broadened their membership from white male Protestants to white male Christians. In fact, they might even have accepted white male Jews—at least if there weren't too many of them—but, for some reason, none seemed eager to join.

Tonight, though, as they sat shoulder to shoulder around the campfire, their leader, Colonel Henry Bumpkin, the owner of the farm, had a special subject to discuss that weighed heavily upon them all. "There's something going on at UAardvark," he began, striding back and forth before them in his full-dress uniform and highly polished boots. "I'm not sure exactly what it is. But from what I've heard there's more people speakin' those strange foreign languages at that place than ever before. What can that mean? Do you think they're A-rabs, Corporal Slobodov?"

Slobodov, never the brightest of lights, was not sure how to respond. "Well, there's a couple o' greasers that works down in the Tunnels. But maybe they're not Mexicans at all. Maybe they're A-rabs. Who can tell 'em apart? They all look the same!"

This inspired lots of murmuring around the campfire, with considerable discussion of whether or not they did all look the same. Also, some Patriots wondered if Mexico was in the Middle East. Others wondered if the Middle East was in Mexico.

Private John McNamara, a secret FBI infiltrator in the Patriot ranks, spoke up and made the point that the foreign language speakers might well be students. "Some students come from foreign countries," he said, "while others are taking foreign language courses."

"You mean they *teach* foreign languages at that place?" screeched the Rev. Billy Ray Jones, a corpulent fundamentalist minister. "What kind of American school is that?!! They should be teaching American students to speak American!"

Outraged voices from around the fire hollered out: "Damn right, Brother Jones. You tell 'em! America for Americans!"

"That is pretty shocking," Colonel Bumpkin agreed. "And what about those foreign students? Why do they admit them in the first place? Right now they're probably going around the USA planting bombs and spreading their Muslim ideology. I've heard, from reliable sources, that Sharia law is already practiced in 26 of the 38 American states. That's why you see so many American women wearing those flimsy, teeny-tiny bathing suits!"

"Yeah!" responded the members of the crowd, turning their thoughts to appetizing visions of women in bikinis.

Sergeant Pete Harris, however, a brawny local security guard, brought up a still graver offense. "What about the War on Christmas?" he demanded. "Has there ever been a big Christmas celebration at UAardvark? Is there ever going to be? I haven't seen any signs of it."

Even Slobodov could spot the flaw in Harris's complaint. So he said: "The campus is closed over Christmas. It's the vacation period, see? No one is there to celebrate."

"That's just it," Sergeant Harris responded heatedly. "Why are they takin' vacations during the most important part of the year, when they could be on campus celebratin' the birth of our Savior, holdin' nativity pageants, and convertin' the heathen? This war on Christmas is clearly a plot by the secular humanists, as well as by the godless Jews and Muslims."

In the midst of a roar of approval from the gathering, Slobodov was forced to acknowledge, shamefacedly, that Sergeant Harris had made some excellent points.

"Yes, when we move onto that campus and restore discipline there," observed Colonel Bumpkin, there'll be plenty o' Christmas celebration, as well as compulsory Bible study and"—here he paused to consider the options—"weekly virginity exams for female students!"

Another roar of approval followed, punctuated by the joyous tossing of empty and half-filled beer bottles into the fire. Sparks rose in a great shower.

"I heared there's lesbians on that campus," the Rev. Jones shouted out, "and homos, too! With that kind of thinkin', no wonder sexuality's runnin' rampant over there. We should just send those lezzies back to where they come from!"

"Where's that?" someone asked.

There was a pause. "Why, Iran, I guess," he said. "Or maybe

it's Afghanistan. Or China. They just send 'em here to undermine America's strength. But we're not gonna let 'em do that, are we, boys?"

The "boys"—belching, cursing, and scratching themselves —swore they wouldn't.

"The real question," said Colonel Bumpkin, "is: what are we gonna do about these and other alarming developments at UAardvark? We could stage a preemptive strike now, usin' our God-fearin' armed might to crush the liberal traitors runnin' that campus. But, at this point, we don't know the full extent of their operations, nor do we know their detailed plans."

"That's right," someone hollered.

"So, as your commander, I hereby authorize the beginnin' of our own fact-findin' mission: Operation America! For the next few weeks, we are goin' to watch that campus real close and gather intelligence information about it. Then, with full knowledge of the conspiracy against our great nation, its brave fighting men, and its cherished values, we will strike!"

Cheers rent the air, while Slobodov, drowned out by the tumult, let loose a particularly large belch.

# Chapter 20

## Night Thoughts

Well after midnight, a brief but fierce spring thunderstorm sent torrential rain, accompanied by wild lightning and crashing thunder, across large portions of the eastern and central United States. Many in Aardvark and elsewhere were awakened by the storm, only to fall back into slumber again after its rapid departure.

Harry Anderson awoke worrying about Jake and his continued deterioration. Would his old friend eventually turn a corner and return to a happy, productive life? Recalling Jake's recent behavior, Harry wasn't sure.

When Ellen Smithers awoke, she found herself also worried about Jake, but even more so about her husband, Frank Collins, who had seemed to be growing sicker over the past week. She looked with concern at Frank, lying beside her in bed. But he seemed to be sleeping peacefully.

In response to the thunder, Marsha Skelton sat bolt upright. She had been having a very intriguing dream in which, as university president, she had been employing Hopkins and past university officials as overworked secretaries. That's the way it should be, she thought, plumping up her pillow and dozing off again.

Meanwhile, in an expensive Virginia suburb not far from the nation's capital, General Buck Thorkelson shifted his substantial bulk to a more comfortable position in his king-sized bed. He had been having a dream about Ms. Zowee's feet. Perhaps, if he concentrated, he could return to it.

In Dallas, William T. Swagger V, rudely awakened by the storm, switched on his bedside lamp and once more checked his iPad. A net worth of $6.6 billion. Not bad! Turning off the light, he lay back and rolled over with a smile on his face.

Back in Aardvark, most members of the poker group were also awake, with their brains spinning out fantasies and questions. Helen Meyerson thought how nice it would be to win Aardvark's lesbian wrestling match, scheduled to begin in four weeks. As he did often, Sam Gates pondered what it would take to stir the American working class to revolt. Gina Sorrentino dreamed of being young, beautiful, and able to turn men's heads once again. As for Selwyn Abernathy, he wondered what it would be like to be received by the royal family at Buckingham Palace.

In the student dorms, which had fallen relatively quiet only about half an hour before, Natasha Randall awoke irritably. Would anything interesting ever happen around this dumb campus? The students, especially, were boring, drunken dolts—although she had to admit that that guy she'd met the other night, Phil, was pretty sharp and kinda cute.

Wilma "The Witch" Welsh, who lived in a dark, shuttered house far from campus, was delighted by the storm, and was sorry it didn't last longer. Arising from her bed, she studied herself carefully in the mirror. Yes, she was both cruel and beautiful, she decided. But, if she was truly to succeed as a witch, she'd have to work on maintaining that green tint.

When the thunder hit, The Crusher sat up in the bedroll

he used when sleeping on the floor of the abandoned house occupied by his motorcycle gang. Stretching his massive, tattooed arms and yawning deeply, he wondered what it would be like to be published in the *International Review of Poetry.*

Many of the cleaning and maintenance workers, having worked hard until well into the evening, were too tired to be awakened by the storm. But their dreams were peppered with visions of working-class heroes that ranged from Spartacus to Eugene Debs. Tom Rowley, though, was a lighter sleeper than most and, before falling back into slumber, decided that the next session in his course on Marx and working-class liberation would focus on Marx's role in the formation of social democratic parties. Eva, too, was awake, and decided to get up and read some more about Rosa Luxemburg in a book she had "borrowed" from Sam Gates's office.

In a different part of town, their supervisor, Stan Slobodov, awoke to the sound of the thunder in a full sweat. For months, a powerful vision had haunted his dreams—a vision of being kicked in the face by a powerful, uniformed, booted leader. It was both a little frightening and, he thought, strangely attractive.

Although Stan lacked the imagination to realize it, Colonel Henry Bumpkin of the Christian Patriots was the fantasy figure of his dream. And, coincidentally, at that very moment, the colonel, awakened by the storm in his home (the Americanism Defense Fortress), was busy visualizing himself as the nation's supreme leader, kicking someone in the face.

The storm also shattered the sleep of UAardvark's president, Dwight Hopkins. He had been dreaming of engaging in secret, painful pleasures with a woman he knew. But she was certainly not his wife, who lay beside him on the bed. Determined not to wake her or to provoke her amorous advances, he kept as still as he could.

Mary Jo Hopkins, who, like her husband, had been awakened by a clap of thunder, did her best to appear asleep. "What is the matter with Dwight?" she wondered. He was handsome, wealthy, and, in some ways, charming—just the sort of man she had been groomed to marry. But, unfortunately, he no longer seemed at all interested in her.

Through it all, Jake Holland slept soundly and with murky dreams. Alone at home, he was, as he would have said, drunk as a skunk. But even if he had been awake, he would have been unable to comprehend the mélange of fantasies, thoughts, and emotions that swirled about UAardvark.

Thus, neither Jake nor anyone else was quite ready for the dramatic events that were about to unfold.

# Chapter 21

## A Big Bummer

The weekend had arrived, and Jake—with no classes to teach and, thus, without qualms of conscience about missing any—was sleeping soundly in his bed that Saturday morning, recovering from a drunken binge the previous night. Unfortunately, the telephone now rang, long and insistently. Eventually, cursing to himself, he managed to pick up the receiver.

"Jake, it's me, Ellen," said the latest love of his life, sounding awful. "He's dead!"

For a short time, Jake's befuddled mind raced wildly, hoping it was someone he really disliked but suspecting that it wasn't. "Who?" he finally croaked, his vocal cords slowly moving into action.

"It's Frank," she said, crying. "I couldn't wake him up this morning. He must have died during the night." She stopped speaking for a time, sobbing, but then continued: "I'm at the hospital, and the doctor here said it must have been a heart attack. Oh, Jake, I knew he was a sick man, but I didn't think he'd die so damned soon!" Here she stopped speaking completely and sobbed hysterically.

"Look Ellen," he said, now fully awake. "You're probably going to head home soon, right?"

She sniffled in reply.

"I'll meet you there in half an hour."

"OK," she said in a weak voice.

Thirty minutes later, Jake arrived at her house, having washed, shaved, and sobered up along the way. Embracing tearfully at the door, they headed inside, where they sat together on the couch.

"Frank was such a good man," she said. "Oh, sure, he could be cantankerous at times. But who wouldn't be, given his physical condition? What was so wonderful about him was that he never stopped fighting those military bastards. He never gave up in the face of hopeless odds. He got local veterans' groups to demand an investigation of the health hazards of using Agent Orange, depleted uranium, and other toxic materials in U.S. weapons. And then he got them to condemn the latest U.S. war plans. In fact, he was getting ready to go to Washington to testify as their spokesman at upcoming Senate hearings."

"Yes, he was terrific," Jake replied, and meant it. He thought sadly that he'd miss Frank almost as much as Ellen would.

"Best of all, though," said Ellen, "Frank never threw in the towel. He never gave up hope for this misbegotten town or for this damned country." Once again she began sobbing, this time so heavily that her entire body shook.

Jake put his arms around her and held her close. It felt great.

But he probably embraced her a bit too long, and, recognizing this, Ellen drew back from him abruptly.

"Sorry," he said, "I guess I held you a little longer than I would The Crusher." Then, in response to Ellen's look of bewilderment, Jake added: "Despite appearances, he's a very sensitive guy."

Ellen smiled for a moment at that idea but, then, suddenly grew more serious. "Jake, I realize that you're being supportive, and I really appreciate that. I know you've always been a good friend of mine, and of Frank's. And I also realize," she said, taking a gulp, "that you've had a crush on me for a long time now."

The room suddenly grew very quiet. Jake stopped breathing.

"But," she continued, "although I like you very much—and even though, now, Frank is no longer here as the man in my life—I'm not going to get romantically involved with you."

Jake, dismayed by this turn of the conversation, said: "It's really Frank, isn't it? Of course, it's much too early for you to be thinking about our relationship, given his death just last night. I'm terribly sorry to have brought up the issue, if only indirectly."

Ellen looked at Jake for a moment. "Actually, that's not it, at all," she said. "I'll always be very fond of you, Jake. Really, in many ways you're a wonderful guy. But, frankly," she added, and then stopped. "Are you sure you want me to continue?"

"Yes, yes," said Jake, feeling his life shutting down.

"Well frankly," she said, looking away from him, "you're burnt out. You've given up. You've become cynical. I need a man in my life who inspires me—not one who depresses me."

A long silence followed. And, after that, they chatted for a few more moments, with Jake barely conscious of what they were saying. "You'll be OK, won't you Jake?" she asked, deeply concerned about the consequences of her blunt remarks.

"Sure, sure," he replied. "Anyway, you're the one who's received the heavier blow, with Frank's death and all."

She nodded, smiling weakly. Then she kissed him goodbye lightly on his cheek and thanked him for coming to her house to comfort her. He waved and headed out to the street.

Driving toward his house, he thought glumly: "Well, I can't

blame her. To be perfectly objective about it, I wouldn't want to get involved with me, either!"

But that thought only made him feel worse. Passing a liquor store, he stopped and bought five bottles of Jack Daniels. There was already plenty in his house, but he figured he'd need some more, sooner or later. "Be prepared! That's the Boy Scouts' marching song," he sang to himself, with his usual gallows humor.

A few minutes later, strolling up the path to his front door, he recalled his meeting with Ellen—holding her in his arms and, a few moments later, listening to her rule him out of her love life. Reaching the door, he looked at it a moment and, then, smashed his right fist into it, splintering the wood.

Once inside, Jake put a bandage on his wounded hand. Then he got down to some serious drinking.

# Chapter 22

## A UAardvark Summit Meeting

In the campus Bank of America Building (formerly the university's Administration Building), President Hopkins called to order a meeting of the top UAardvark administrators.

Although this building housed a luxurious conference room, Hopkins preferred holding such gatherings on the penthouse level, in the rejuvenatron, which housed today's meeting. Purchased for what the administration considered a bargain price of $14.6 million, the rejuvenatron was a very expensive tanning, fat-removing, ab-hardening, hair-, genital-, and bowel-improvement device that accommodated up to 15 people comfortably. Over the past decade, the administration had grown rapidly, and now outnumbered the faculty. As a result, at the moment there were 20 top administrators crowding into the gadget. Aside from President Hopkins, they included the vice president for memoranda, the vice president for surveys, the vice president for surveillance, the vice president for computer games, the vice president for sales, the vice president for men's rooms, the vice president for ladies' rooms, and the vice president for vice presidents. Unfortunately, there was no room for the many associate vice presidents and the assistant vice presidents. But a substantially larger rejuvenatron had been ordered for $23.8 million and, until it arrived, the minutes of this gathering would have to suffice for these lower-ranking officials.

The lucky few who had been admitted to the rejuvenatron wore bathing suits and sat in pools of warm, oily water, with only the upper portions of their bodies exposed to the air. The water was highly scented, a feature that presumably helped restore nasal passages. Many of the participants wore gold chains around their necks, adorned with the initials of their names. This style, born in the nation's black ghettoes, had become increasingly popular within the ranks of university administrators, who competed with one another in the size and design of the initials.

"Before we begin," Hopkins said, "who will take the minutes?"

"Not I," said the vice president for hallways.

"Not I," said the vice president for bulletin boards.

"Not I," said the vice president for parking.

"Jesus," thought Hopkins. "These guys get paid an average of half a million bucks a year, and they can't even take notes at a meeting!" He glared at them until the vice president for plumbing, eager to ingratiate himself with his boss, volunteered for the job. "Thank you, Jenkins," Hopkins said.

"It's Smith, sir. And it's a pleasure to serve you."

"Jenkins, Smith, whatever," remarked Hopkins. "Remind me of your service the next time merit raises come around."

"Yes, sir!" replied the vice president for plumbing, as his fellow vice presidents threw dirty glances at him and fingered their gold initials nervously.

"Let's turn to the first major item of business," said the president. "I have received a report from the Committee on University Restructuring—an off-campus team developed for us by the Chase Manhattan Bank. This report, entitled *The Well-Managed University of the Future*, recommends eliminating all liberal arts departments on campus, thus terminating about one-half of the faculty. A small portion of those terminated would be offered part-time positions, at a tiny fraction of their past salaries. You can imagine what a terrific financial savings this will mean for UAardvark! Although the study cost $7.9 million, it was well worth it! Anyway, the upshot is that I will begin implementing the committee's plan this fall."

"What a wonderful idea, Mr. President!" declared the vice president for vice presidents, widely viewed as the second-in-command on campus and, therefore, always the first to respond to President Hopkins.

"Yes, yes," said the vice president for file cabinets. "That money could be used much more economically and efficiently than on useless frills like languages, literature, history, and the like."

"Exactly what I was thinking, Brown," replied Hopkins.

"Er, it's Trewick, Mr. President."

"Whatever," replied Hopkins dismissively, smoothing back his perfect silver hair and turning to a new issue.

"I'm sorry to report that I have a further matter to discuss with you—a very unpleasant one," he began. "One of our faculty members, Ellen Smithers, a professor of women's studies—whatever that is—is at the center of it. Do any of you know her?"

No one did, for high-level administrators rarely, if ever, spoke with faculty or, for that matter, with students.

"Well," Hopkins continued, "Professor Smithers has been attempting to destroy the university by filing a Freedom of Information Act request with the federal government for information on our very own New Technology Center. Fortunately, though, I have friends in government positions who have not only blocked this request but also informed me of it so that the university can take appropriate action. Consequently, at tomorrow's faculty meeting I will announce that she has been fired and must vacate her classroom and office immediately."

A wave of applause, although a bit damp and oily, swept through the throng of administrators.

"Can we sue her?" asked the vice president for surveillance.

"No, that would appear vindictive," said the president. "And, also, our lawyers point out that a lawsuit against her has no legal basis. But I think that, by taking the action I have outlined, we will have made an example of her that will discourage other faculty from interfering with our forward-looking university plans— for example, the plan to eliminate the liberal arts departments."

"Brilliant thinking, Mr. President!" hollered the vice president for plumbing, anxious to cement his new relationship with Hopkins. But, although Hopkins smiled in pleasure, the others in the rejuvenatron, recognizing this remark as crass opportunism, glared at the vice president and merely applauded politely.

"Finally," said President Hopkins, "I am pleased to report that businesses are finding our New Technology Center increasingly appealing. Alas, I can't report yet on a wonderful arrangement I am working out with a giant corporation. But suffice it to say that this arrangement will bring in very large amounts of money to cover our vital expenses. In this connection, I already have been thinking about the appointment of additional administrators— and perhaps advancing some of you to the status of executive vice president."

As cheers filled the air, Hopkins leaned over and pressed a

button on the wall. Speakers in the corners of the rejuvenatron immediately began booming out the university fight song, "On UAardvark." Satisfied that things had gone well, he closed the meeting with a crisp salute to the assemblage.

These were good men and women, he thought to himself. Some day he would have to learn their names.

# Chapter 23

## Jake's Renaissance

It was late Monday afternoon and, although Jake heard a pounding on his front door, he was determined not to move. Having fallen asleep in a drunken stupor that morning on his living room couch, he had no desire to make his way to the door, or even to fully wake up. "Let the intruder depart," he muttered, as he settled himself more comfortably on the couch.

But the pounder was maddeningly persistent, and ultimately Jake arose, cursing, and headed for the door.

It was Harry.

"Damn it, Harry, I was sleeping," said Jake, leaning for support on the doorframe.

"Well it's time to wake up, man," Harry retorted. "It's almost five in the afternoon, and I have some important news for you."

Resigned to living in the cruel world of wakefulness, Jake motioned him in and asked: "Drink?"

"No, Jake. And you might want to sober up a bit, too," Harry said, as Jake shrugged and flopped back on the couch. "I've just come from a faculty meeting—chaired, of course, by the inimitable Dwight Hopkins."

"I thought you said this was important," Jake began, his sense of humor starting to peep through once more.

"Oh, it is. It is," said Harry. "Just listen. At the meeting Hopkins unveiled a splendid new administration plan, with implementation to begin in the fall, that will simply eliminate all liberal arts departments. Some of the affected faculty will then be hired back on a part-time, contingent basis. That way, the rehired faculty will lose most of their salary and all of their benefits, while the rest of those terminated will simply lose everything."

"Not so good for the faculty, is it?" asked Jake, attempting to sit up.

"No, it's not—although it's being lauded by the administration as great for the university," said Harry, "for it saves a lot of money that can be used for 'important' things. You know, things like a new rejuvenatron, more administrators, and the New Technology Center."

"Ah, yes. Worthy projects. Can't get enough of those," said Jake, finally managing to sit upright. "And how are our colleagues on the faculty taking this news?"

"There was general consternation, but no one spoke up. Neither you, Sam, nor Gina was on the scene. Our peerless union leader, The Witch, *was* there, but she said nothing."

"Of course," said Jake, waving his hand in the air. Wilma, after all, was hopeless. "But you know, Harry," he continued, with a frown, "we invited this. By letting these slick administrators turn this campus into a shopping center, by letting them ride roughshod over us for years, we deserved this. And now we've got it."

Harry, not quite as willing to accept responsibility for this disaster, responded with a trace of annoyance: "Did Ellen deserve it, too?"

"What do you mean?" asked Jake, suddenly alert.

Harry looked him in the eyes. "I didn't mention it, but toward the end of the meeting Hopkins announced that Ellen was being fired as of today. According to his official statement, she had been destroying the university. But the scuttle is that what did her in was a Freedom of Information Act request."

"They fired Ellen?" Jake asked, in disbelief. "^#%%$%(^! And within days of Frank's death, too. Those bastards!"

"Frank's death probably wasn't part of the administration's calculations, one way or the other," said Harry. "It was her FOIA request and, according to gossip, the administration's desire to keep us in line. Showing us who's boss."

Both friends grew silent.

Harry finally rose to his feet. "Anyway, Jake, I've got to head on home. But a lot of people are upset by all of this, especially the plan to terminate their jobs. So you might want to give some thought to whether there's anything we can do about it. After all, you're a longtime political agitator, with more experience along these lines than most of us have. If that whiskey hasn't pickled your brain, maybe you can come up with some ideas about how we can block the plans of Hopkins and his crew."

But, as Harry went out the door, Jake just stared into space, dazed by what he had heard about Ellen. As the evening came on and darkened the room, he continued to sit on the couch, recovering from the shock but growing progressively angrier. "Those bastards," he muttered over and over. "Pompous, overpaid idiots, with no respect for knowledge or education." And they had fired Ellen for investigating their corporate shenanigans. Sweet, wonderful Ellen.

Eventually, he got up and, turning on a lamp, began pacing around the room. His eyes lit on the books arrayed on his shelves. The collected writings of Voltaire. The memoirs of

Bertrand Russell. A biography of Emma Goldman. Another on the life of Eugene Debs. The novels of Jack London. John Steinbeck's *The Grapes of Wrath*. "What would they be doing in these circumstances?" he wondered. Well, that was a pretty dumb question. They'd get out there and organize resistance. He sighed, and went back to pacing.

Of course, he could console himself with the fact that he didn't have such a bad track record when it came to resistance. He glanced at a peace poster on his wall, as well as at a photograph taken of him on a union picket line, holding a placard saying "Solidarity Forever." There weren't many faculty members, including those who were undoubtedly scurrying about now, worried about the end of their departments, who could match that.

But, noting the whiskey bottles scattered about the room, he suddenly felt ashamed. Who was he kidding? He hadn't done anything politically meaningful for years. It was Ellen who had kept the spark of activism alive on campus, even when she lacked the tenured status that might have given her some protection from retaliation. And, naturally, the administration had fired her. Bastards! Bastards!

Jake returned to his angry pacing, and, then, suddenly, in mid-room, he stopped. Enough of this already! Starting in the living room and proceeding through the rest of the house, he methodically gathered his bottles of whiskey and placed them next to the kitchen sink. Then, one by one, he emptied their contents down the drain. It took quite a while. "Sorry, fish," he said, with a grim smile. "I hate to flood your environment with all this alcohol. But I've got some important work to do."

# Chapter 24

## A Revolt Takes Shape

The following evening, the poker group assembled at the Galway for its regular game.

Gina was in a particularly good mood, having begun a new love affair, although she refused to say with whom. Selwyn, too, was upbeat, announcing that it was Prince Philip's birthday. Jake, though, ultimately drew the group's attention, for, in place of his usual whiskey, there stood a glass of sparkling water.

"Going on the wagon, Jake?" asked Helen, pointing to the glass as she dealt the cards.

"Well, you never know," said Jake. In fact, he hadn't touched a drop of alcohol since he poured gallons of it down the drain the previous day. And he was not intending to again. Breaking the long-term habit was a strain—in fact, an ordeal—and he could feel his body screaming in protest at the abrupt change. But now, he realized, was not the time to talk about it. Instead, he quipped: "Anyway, back in my homeland of the Bronx, everyone except the *goyim* viewed seltzer as a kind of health food."

"In your case, I'm sure it is," Sam remarked sardonically. "Anyway, we should all probably get ready for new lives—or maybe deaths—now that the administration's axe is falling on our necks."

"Yes, wasn't that an incredible speech the other day by our boy Hopkins?" said Harry. "It looks like our days at UAardvark are numbered. And his contempt for the liberal arts, the very foundation of higher education, is unbelievable—although, given his overall approach, I guess it's not really surprising."

They paused to make their bets, after which Helen dealt them each another card.

Having glanced at his cards and wincing, Selwyn looked up and said: "The whole thing is deplorable. And, once again, we're caught flatfooted by the administration, without any effective way to respond. If we had a union worth its salt, maybe we'd have a chance, but. . . ." He threw up his hands.

"Oh, so now you decide you'd like a powerful union," Helen said.

"Well, anything would be better than this," Selwyn countered.

Everyone nodded glumly.

"What do you think, Jake?" asked Sam. "Any ideas?"

"Yes," said Jake, looking up from his cards. Pausing a bit for emphasis, he said: "I think we should throw the bastards out!"

Laughing and snorting, the others tossed crumpled napkins, beer coasters, and whatever else they had handy at him. Helen cried out: "Get serious, man!"

Jake responded slowly: "I am serious." And, suddenly, unexpectedly, it was clear that he was.

"Look," he said, leaning forward. "Half the faculty is on the verge of being either fired or turned into part-time servants. And the other half must realize that it no longer has any job security. We have nothing to lose by staging a rebellion—not just a revolt to block this particular plan, but a revolt to get rid of the entire horrible crew of administrators."

The room grew silent, as the poker hands were deposited on the table.

"Furthermore," said Jake, "we can win. After all, we're smarter than they are. Much smarter. Don't you think we have enough brains and creativity to bring down that clown in the president's office and his circle of overpaid ass-kissers?"

"Yes, yes, Jake," Gina said, her eyes shining.

"%(^^_(#* right," said Sam.

Selwyn added: "And even if we don't win, it could be a lot of fun."

Everyone nodded in agreement.

"OK, so here's how I think we should do it," Jake said.

"Wait a minute!" Harry cried out, laughing with delight. "You had all this worked out before coming here, didn't you?"

"Well, I did give it some thought," Jake admitted, as the remaining napkins were thrown at him.

"Anyway," he said, "step one: We constitute ourselves the steering committee of a UAardvark campus revolt. Step two: We plan a period of heightening anti-administration chaos on the campus, designed to garner media attention, alienate the administration's constituencies from the administration, and mobilize support from the campus community. Day after day, there will be new, sensational events. I figure that the six of us can each take responsibility for organizing one of them. Then we can work collectively on organizing the seventh."

There was a pause, as the others took in the seriousness and breadth of the action plan.

Eventually, Helen said: "It's beautiful, Jake." Others nodded their agreement. "But we need to start soon, as we're nearing the end of the semester."

"Yes, we should move rapidly on this," said Jake. "As I've had more time than the rest of you to think about this stuff, I suggest that I kick things off the day after tomorrow with a surprise at the university's Corporate Celebration Day."

"And maybe I could be ready with a little something the next day, when the top administrators will be meeting with a group of well-heeled alumni," remarked Gina.

In fact, Jake's enthusiasm was infectious, and soon the others, too, began to stake out days and toss around ideas for action.

"You realize," said Jake, "that we're going to have to meet regularly, probably nightly, to discuss and coordinate our plans."

"Yes!" the others cried, clearly excited and more than ready to get going.

"Also, of course," said Harry, "these plans must be kept totally secret. One of our greatest strengths is our ability to take the administration by surprise."

Jake agreed. "Yes, consider yourselves sworn to secrecy." Then, lifting his glass, he cried: "To the UAardvark campus revolt. *Venceremos!*"

Spontaneously, they all leaped to their feet and raised their glasses: "*Venceremos!*"

Tears sprang to the eyes of some, and they all hugged one another—delighted, after years of feeling like helpless victims, to be taking action. For a time, a happy silence enveloped the room.

Finally, Gina spoke up. "I hate to break the spell. But can we get back to our poker game? I don't want to give up this hand."

"Sure," said Sam, as he and the others settled back in their seats. "Let's do that. This might be our last poker night for a while."

# Chapter 25

## Corporate Celebration Day

Corporate Celebration Day dawned warm and sunny that April, with the UAardvark campus looking quite verdant. Flowers had been specially planted for the event, and patches of grass that appeared rather brown had been spray-painted green. Large, colorful banners with corporate logos hung over the entrances. "Welcome to UAardvark's Corporate Celebration Day!" they proclaimed. The local community had been invited to participate, and invitations had gone out to the major U.S. corporations to send representatives. After all, the idea of the event was not only to publicize the business-friendly climate already established on campus, but also to attract even more corporate involvement. About 500 chairs had been set up outdoors in the J.P. Morgan Quadrangle, and hundreds more lay at hand, in case an overflow crowd turned up. A small stage, also adorned with corporate logos, had been erected in front, with a podium and microphone. White-coated waiters stood ready to serve champagne and a variety of hors d'oeuvres.

Jake watched on the sidelines as the crowd began filtering in. "Will everything work as planned?" he wondered. The official program called for a short speech of welcome by President Hopkins, followed by welcoming statements volunteered by faculty, students, and members of the community. It presented an interesting opportunity, Jake knew, and he just hoped the people he had lined up would use it effectively.

Suddenly the ear-splitting roar of engines filled the air,

and several dozen Hells Angels motorcyclists rode into view. The Daffodil Poetry Club (formerly the Kickass Avengers) had arrived.

Jake relaxed. The fun was about to begin.

Startled by the arrival of the menacing-looking cyclists, the crowd gave way as the brawny, black leather-clad, heavily spiked figures, some wearing military helmets and all sporting violent tattoos, strode up to the waiters, seized drinks, and helped themselves to the lion's share of the food. Not all of the cyclists were men, but the women among them—some missing teeth and all displaying hefty biceps—looked at least as dangerous. After the cyclists seated themselves in the front rows, the rest of the crowd gravitated several rows to the rear.

Ever the master of social situations, President Hopkins kicked off the event by smiling broadly, welcoming the guests to the campus for Corporate Celebration Day, and giving a short speech on the natural harmony of interests between universities and big business. The crowd, including the cyclists, applauded politely.

Then the assorted campus and community statements began. To Jake's delight, no faculty members bothered to speak, and only one student—totally incoherent—gave a little talk, leaving plenty of time for community involvement. A substantial number of the cyclists now lined up at the microphone, with the rest of them forming a phalanx in front of the stage.

The Crusher led off by explaining that they had been studying poetry, most recently by feminist women. "That means that they don't take any ^%(&^)* from ^)*&^ men," he explained. Wide-eyed, the crowd nodded obediently. "But today, to celebrate the

%&^%( corporations," he said, "we've written some haiku in the style of Elizabeth Hughes. You're on, guys."

Sal the Bear stepped forward and led off with his haiku:

Hail our great BP
Bringing the Gulf your oil
What a tasty dish.

The audience applauded politely. Big Frankie then read his own original work:

O Dow Chemical
The Vietnamese remember
Your burning napalm.

Applause again followed, but this time more restrained. Angela ("The Nutcracker") Fillipi then strode to the podium, reading:

How grateful we are
To Bank of America
For taking our home.

The audience, now growing jittery, was beginning to wonder if these poems really were meant in praise. Meanwhile, the poetry continued with a haiku by another hulking cyclist, Harry ("Godzilla") Olafson:

Great Union Carbide

In Bhopal, your deeds remain
But you have gone home.

At this point, some members of the audience began standing up and heading out of the quadrangle. Jake noticed that they were all wearing suits and ties. "Probably the corporate guests," he concluded. "Good!" Meanwhile, Alice ("The Hammer") Schultz took the mic and read:

Sweet Coca-Cola
That murders union leaders
Brings good things to death.

The trickle of suits moving away from the gathering was now turning into a flood. But the raggedy-looking younger people in the audience, undoubtedly students, were staying and enjoying the event. Jake noticed his student, Natasha, among them. They applauded wildly as Harvey ("Tiny") Belinski, a muscle-bound, 300-pound behemoth with a shaven head and a patch over one eye, launched into his contribution to the celebration:

The path to wisdom
Is fair and balanced Fox News
As good as *Pravda*.

Although the quadrangle had largely emptied out by this point, the fleeing attendees didn't get very far, for six huge trucks, driven by members of the Daffodil Poetry Club, blocked the campus roads and exits. Some of the trucks had flat tires, while others had become jammed into narrow turning areas, thus leaving them immobile. Adding to the blockage, hundreds of cars driven by attendees fleeing Corporate Celebration Day were now part of a massive traffic jam that filled campus roads to such an extent that they had become impassable.

Frantic at this turn of events, administrators ordered campus police to clear the roads. But the campus police—a crew of elderly men who had retired from their regular law enforcement jobs in the surrounding communities to take an easy job on campus—had no desire to provoke the bikers. Nor could they think of any way to untangle the traffic jam. In desperation, the administration called upon the Aardvark town police to clear the area. But these law enforcement officials, arriving in their cars and confronting a vast jumble of huge trucks and cars, found no practicable way to get onto the campus.

In the midst of this gridlock, the bikers easily wove their motorcycles through the maze of stranded cars and distributed copies of their haiku to the passengers. They were also interviewed by stranded reporters from the *Aardvark Enterprise*, the town radio station, and the town television station, who told the delighted bikers that they and their haiku would be featured in the stories they filed.

As things turned out, the traffic jam on campus continued for the next four hours—more than enough time to create apoplexy among administrators, seething anger among corporate representatives, and amusement among students, who (lying about on the grass and smoking pot) watched in joyous disbelief.

Meeting that evening at the Galway, Jake and his fellow

conspirators couldn't have been happier. It was a fine debut to the revolt on campus. And Gina, grinning mischievously, promised that tomorrow would be even better.

# Chapter 26

## The Alumni Luncheon

After the previous day's disaster, the UAardvark administration was hoping for a comeback with a special alumni luncheon scheduled in the university's Haynes Underwear Banquet Hall. For the past few years, the vice president for alumni donations had been compiling information on the wealthiest graduates of UAardvark. Using a list of those he believed to be the very richest, referred to in administration circles as "The Top 100," his office had worked out a plan with President Hopkins to invite them to a lavish banquet designed to charm them into making substantial financial contributions to the university. They would receive engraved invitations to the event, at which they would be lauded for their "accomplishments" by Hopkins and served a special luncheon.

As the well-dressed alumni arrived at the banquet hall in their limousines, Bugattis, Ferraris, Porsches, Mercedes, Rolls-Royces, and Lamborghinis, they were greeted at the door by 12 vice presidents, who ushered them into a pre-luncheon cocktail hour in the large United Brands Room. Here they chatted with additional vice presidents and associate vice presidents, as well as with a small number of faculty members. The faculty had been invited by the administration to attend the reception, but not the far more expensive luncheon.

At the reception, President Hopkins gave a short welcoming address, and informed the alumni that, as exemplars of the university at its best, they would be served a very unique meal—genetically modified food produced under the direction of chemists from the Monsanto Corporation in the university's own Monsanto School of Science. "Environmentalist kooks have whined for years about genetically-modified crops," he explained, "but you will soon learn how absolutely delicious such food can be!" Clapping with delight, the wealthy alumni drank to the university and the inspiring leadership of President Hopkins.

Only a few faculty members, as they circulated among the alumni, suggested a somewhat different interpretation of the food that would be served, although their critique was subtle. "I'm sure the meal will be delicious," one faculty member remarked to a porcine woman, dripping with diamonds. "But, of course, this is the first time it has been served."

Another elderly professor told one of his former students, now a prominent banker: "Although it would be tempting to overeat, you really shouldn't. It's possible that these new foods might create a bit of a tummy ache."

Suddenly, the waiters threw open the great doors of the dining room. Led by President Hopkins and Henry Simpson, the president of the Alumni Association, the alumni and administrators filed in, while the faculty, having outlived their usefulness, filed out.

As President Hopkins had suggested, the food did taste very good, and the diners scarfed it down happily. After about 30 minutes, President Hopkins rose, smiling, and began to address the gathering. "Alumni of UAardvark," he began, "we are delighted to have you with us today, honoring your magnificent achievements in business, finance, and . . . and other areas of endeavor." The audience applauded, although he noticed that some alumni seemed distracted, and one or two ran out the door. Shrugging it off, he continued: "Today, some seem to think it a mark of shame when an individual acquires great wealth. Well, I want to assure you that we at UAardvark do not think so. Indeed," he said, establishing the eye contact that he used when he wanted to appear sincere, "we believe that the wealthy are the best and the brightest, the very backbone of the American way of life."

But then he stopped. Something was definitely wrong. Several alumni were staggering toward the doors. Two others seemed to have vomited on their tables.

Outside, at the side door to the kitchen, one of the cooks emerged and lit a cigarette. Gina, who had been waiting for this moment, walked up to him. "How's it going, Ricardo?" she asked.

"It's started," he said with a grin.

The previous day, Gina had spoken with Ricardo, an underpaid kitchen worker, and urged him to spike the banquet's salad dressing with ipecac, a surefire producer of vomiting. At the time, she had thought he would need some convincing. But he hadn't. "No problem," he had said. "In fact, it will be a pleasure."

Meanwhile, inside the dining hall, chaos reigned. About half the alumni and administrators were now vomiting with great vigor, including President Hopkins. Noticing that Henry Simpson, the Alumni Association president, was one of them, the vice president for vice presidents rushed up to him with a napkin and tried to clean him off, only to end up vomiting on the alumni president himself. Even people who had not touched the salad dressing were sickened by the sight and smell of vomit everywhere, and ultimately began vomiting themselves.

The men's and ladies' rooms were soon filled with diners vomiting into the sinks and toilets or, when they could not reach them, on the floor. In their desperation, several men ran into the ladies' room, shoving women aside to get to the sinks. Infuriated, the mass of women counterattacked, shoving the faces of the male intruders into the vomit-filled sinks and toilet bowls.

With no help to be found in the building, the enraged alumni scrambled for their cars, screaming obscenities and swearing that they would sue the university for everything it had. Those moguls of the mass media in attendance shook their fists and promised that Hopkins would rue the day that he was born.

Observing this precipitous departure, Gina and Ricardo knew that they must have done something right.

* * *

Later that afternoon, having stopped vomiting and having been hosed off by the grounds staff, Hopkins met, dripping, with his inner circle of vice presidents to plan a public relations defense. He desperately wanted to pin the blame for that day's disaster on Monsanto. But that was politically impossible, he knew, as that corporation might then withdraw its huge investments in the university. Therefore, he and other administrators ultimately came out with a press release declaring that the banquet had not, after all, been prepared under the direction of Monsanto.

Instead, claimed the press release, the luncheon had been catered by Le Bourgeois, the fanciest restaurant in the region.

After Hopkins was quoted to that effect in the evening edition of the *Aardvark Enterprise,* the management of Le Bourgeois promptly sued the university for $11 million in damages. This action brought the total demanded in that day's lawsuits against the university to well over $257 million.

Of course, this was not the only consequence of the day's events. That evening, the Aardvark television station ran a lengthy news item, "The University Becomes a Vomitorium," with numerous pictures of alumni fleeing the building covered with vomit. So sensational was this news story that it could not be suppressed. Nor did the national TV networks, influenced by irate alumni, want to suppress it. As a result, news of the event was broadcast all across the United States and the world.

UAardvark was acquiring an international reputation— although not quite the kind the administration wanted.

# Chapter 27

## A Different Luncheon

O n the same day that the alumni gathering erupted in such a conspicuous fashion, a different, more discrete luncheon was taking place at a small, off-campus restaurant.

It brought together two old friends: Helen Meyerson (one of the poker conspirators) and Marsha Skelton (President Hopkins's secretary). A longtime lesbian, Helen had had a passionate affair a decade before with Marsha. Although it lasted less than a year, the two women remained friendly and got together occasionally for lunch, gossip, and a discussion of their current lives.

Today's luncheon meeting, however, had been instigated by Helen because the conspirators were anxious to find out more about the New Technology Center. When Ellen's Freedom of Information Act request failed to generate any useful material along these lines, it was necessary to uncover a new route to the information. And Marsha, at least potentially, might provide them with that—although she didn't know it yet.

During most of the meal, the two women addressed lighter topics.

"Who's that young woman I saw you with at the movies?" Helen asked.

"Oh, Helen," Marsha said. "She's just a neighbor. It's nothing serious."

"So you say, Marsha. But you looked awfully smitten with her."

"Give me a break, Helen," said Marsha, rolling her eyes at her. "At my age, I'm not in the market for romance anymore. And anyway, no one could replace you." She took Helen's hand, and, for a moment, both of them grew teary eyed.

Not surprisingly, they couldn't resist discussing Corporate Celebration Day, and the two of them had a good laugh at what had happened on campus.

"You should have seen the looks on the faces of those corporate guys when those wild-looking Hells Angels started reading poetry that trashed their businesses," said Helen. "I'm sure they'll remember that event for a long time."

"Those smooth corporate operators certainly deserved it," Marsha said, still chuckling. "And that ignorant boss of mine . . . well, anything he sponsors has to result in catastrophe, doesn't it? Though I didn't expect it to happen so fast!"

Again the two women burst into laughter.

Helen felt that the moment was ripe. "Tell me, Marsha, what's behind this mysterious New Technology Center?"

"Oh, it's another 'business-friendly' venture organized by our beloved president," Marsha told her, as she stirred sugar into her second glass of iced tea. "If a corporation wants to have something done there, it merely has to offer the university enough money, and everything is arranged accordingly. Of course, as you might expect, the New Technology Center has absolutely no educational value."

"Why is it all so secret, though?" Helen persisted. "After all, while that arrangement's deplorable, it's not unusual around here, is it?"

"Well, between you and me," said Marsha, "there are some

plans for the center that are really over the top. Quite disgusting, in fact."

"Such as what?" asked Helen.

Looking around her before she replied, Marsha leaned forward slowly and whispered: "Such as storing large quantities of nuclear waste. From the paperwork, it looks like it came from a nuclear weapons explosion." Seeing Helen's jaw drop, Marsha added: "This is all top secret, of course. You can't talk about it to anyone."

Helen was quiet for a moment, and then said: "Marsha, we've got to stop this plan from going forward. You're a physicist. You know how dangerous radioactive material is. How can we allow it to be dumped right in the middle of our university campus? We've got an obligation to expose what's going on to the people who work and study here."

Marsha twisted her napkin uneasily. "Of course this whole thing is terrible," she admitted. "But, if I reveal it, I'm sure to be fired. Whistleblowers don't have an easy time in this society. For God's sake, look at what's happened to Ellen Smithers—a *white* woman—just for requesting information."

"Yes, Ellen was fired. But that's one more reason why we should expose this. How can we let these slick bastards continue to get away with the kinds of things they do?"

"Well, they do get away with an awful lot," Marsha admitted, shaking her head in disgust. "Hopkins would sell his grandmother if he could rake in some additional money doing it. And those vice presidents. There must be hundreds of them, drawing enormous salaries, and doing virtually nothing—or at least nothing useful. All they do is fawn on Hopkins, while he fawns on a bunch of reactionary businessmen. What a crew!"

"So what are we going to do about it, Marsha?" Helen asked, looking her in the eyes. "And especially about this New Technology Center that's going to serve as a nuclear waste dump? If we don't expose this for what it is, we might just as well reconcile ourselves to working at Walmart or some other business enterprise, peddling its shoddy goods."

Marsha grew silent for a while, and finally said: "Look, Helen. You're right—as you sometimes are!" Both women laughed. "But I'm still not sure I want to risk going public myself." Then, after a long pause, she smiled and said: "Suppose I make copies of the key documents from Hopkins's files about the nuclear waste arrangement and, then, deliver them to you?"

"That would be great," Helen replied. "But what should I do with them?"

"Oh, you'll probably think of something," Marsha said with a smile. "I have the sneaking suspicion that you, and maybe others, are up to some mischief around the campus. In fact," she added, "I'll bet you invited me here with the intention of finding out something about the New Technology Center."

It was Helen's turn to feel embarrassed.

"But that's OK, sweetie," Marsha added. "You're right to be suspicious about it. And I'm happy to help out."

"Thanks," said Helen, fondly. "You know, I was just wondering: Why did we ever break up?"

"I don't know," Marsha replied. "Maybe we weren't old enough yet to be thoroughly out of our minds."

# Chapter 28

# The Press Conference

By the following day, numerous reporters from the national TV networks, as well as from major newspapers, were residing at the Strand, Aardvark's largest hotel, seeking to develop follow-up stories about developments at the university. Examining recent events, they began to turn out dispatches that dwelled not only on the bizarre alumni luncheon, but also on the scrapping of the liberal arts departments and the ill-fated Corporate Celebration Day. The university administration, however, remained tight-lipped, issuing bland pronouncements that left reporters dissatisfied and, eventually, unable to add anything new to "the news."

At 5:15 p.m., however, the reporters received phone calls, tweets, emails, and messages faxed on university stationery inviting them to a UAardvark press conference that would be held at 6:00 p.m. in a private room at the hotel. According to the messages, the university's vice president for crises, Dr. Myron Murgatroyd, was going to make a statement of great importance. Scrambling to reach the room promptly and set up their audio and video equipment, the reporters had little time to check out the veracity of the messages. Even if they had, however, university offices were closed for the day and Dr. Murgatroyd was not listed in the phone book.

In fact, Dr. Murgatroyd did not exist. And the university did not have a vice president for crises.

When the reporters were seated in the conference room

and questioning one another about what might be going on, a distinguished-looking individual entered the room from the rear and stepped up to the podium. It was Selwyn Abernathy of the UAardvark campus conspirators. Having closely followed the exploits of the Yes Men, a group of zany individuals who ridiculed corporate malfeasance by impersonating official spokesmen, Selwyn had decided to make this same strategy central to his portion of the campus revolt. He was confident that he could carry off today's performance, for he had a background in the theater. Also, he was well disguised with a wig and makeup. Just in case he had difficulties, though, several members of the poker group were in the audience, ready to spirit him out of the room.

"Ladies and gentlemen," he began, as lights flashed and network TV cameras rolled. "The unfortunate events of the past two days have highlighted, for all to see, problems that are endemic at UAardvark and are visible at all too many colleges and universities around this country. The purpose of a college or university is to advance civilization by drawing upon learned individuals to pursue knowledge, to transmit it throughout the world, and to train students to learn and think, thereby advancing the intellectual progress of humanity."

The jaded audience nodded impatiently, wondering where this hopelessly "old-fashioned" rhetoric was leading.

"Alas," he continued, "in many ways we have not lived up to that great task. Indeed, we have too often perverted education, putting it at the service of business interests—most notably corporations, which have no goal other than to enrich themselves. For education, we have substituted commercial pursuits and mindless television programs. Furthermore, we have elevated administration, which should be no more than a matter of record-keeping and physical plant maintenance, over scholarship and the development of critical thinking. This betrayal of knowledge, this abandonment of wisdom, this cheapening of civilization itself, must not continue," he said. "*And it will not continue at UAardvark!*"

The reporters, jolted awake, scribbled furiously while cameramen focused on Dr. Murgatroyd's stern face.

"On behalf of the university," he said, "I hereby announce that the plan for terminating the liberal arts departments at UAardvark is now withdrawn. Second, construction of the New Technology Center will be halted pending a thorough examination by the faculty of plans for it. Third, all corporate names and logos will be removed from university buildings, and such buildings will henceforth be named after outstanding intellectuals. Fourth, all television sets and commercial products will be removed from the campus. Fifth, the number of administrators will be reduced by 90 percent, and the salaries of the remainder will not be allowed to rise above that of the average faculty member.

"Ladies and gentlemen, that is all I have to say. But I think you will find it sufficient. Copies of my statement can be found on the table by the door. I will not be taking questions." And with that, Dr. Murgatroyd strode out the rear door of the room.

With his departure, the room erupted in pandemonium. A few reporters raced out the door in pursuit of Dr. Murgatroyd, but he was already gone. Others, grabbing a copy of his statement, scrambled from the room as fast as they could to file their stories or to transmit their video footage to the television networks. Some tried phoning the university administration for comment, but couldn't locate any administrators on campus. A few secretaries, in response to questions about Dr. Murgatroyd, did try to be helpful, but said, with regret, that they couldn't possibly keep track of all the administrators at UAardvark. Several of the more industrious reporters tried phoning the residence of President Hopkins. His wife, however, replied that he wasn't home.

Thus, early that evening, Dr. Murgatroyd's spectacular announcement was carried on TV news and opinion shows around the country. Fox News declared that it clearly reflected the fact that Democrats and other leftwing extremists had taken over on the nation's campuses, and had to be stopped before they thoroughly polluted the minds of the nation's youth. By contrast, MSNBC was certain that it was a response to a Republican power-grab, and augured well for the election of the Democratic presidential candidate. Some CNN commentators said that Murgatroyd's announcement showed that American universities were experiencing difficulties, while other commentators said that it showed that they were not.

Arriving home later that evening, Hopkins received a frantic phone call from his vice president for vice presidents, informing him of the incident. "Who the hell is this Murgatroyd guy?" Hopkins stormed. "I didn't know we had a vice president for crises—although it probably wouldn't be a bad idea." After the vice president for vice presidents patiently explained to Hopkins that there was no university vice president for crises—indeed, that Murgatroyd was an imposter—the two men drafted a statement that they immediately dispatched to the mass media.

Quoting Hopkins, the official UAardvark statement declared that the liberal arts departments would be terminated as planned, that construction of the New Technology Center would continue, that corporate names and logos would (of course) be retained on campus buildings, that television sets and commercial products were vital for a modern university, and that campus administrators were already few in number and underpaid. Dr. Murgatroyd was a charlatan, Hopkins explained, as evident from his outlandish comments about the role of a university.

When the networks dutifully reported the UAardvark administration's official response in their late news broadcasts, Hopkins and his fellow administrators hoped that would be the last of the issue. But it was not. Apparently, polls showed that a substantial portion of the American public, especially faculty members at major universities, approved of Dr. Murgatroyd's statement and were appalled by the administration's response to it.

\* \* \*

One of Dr. Murgatroyd's fans was Natasha Randall, who had watched the television broadcasts about UAardvark in Phil's dorm room. Sprawling on a couch with him, Natasha said: "That was one of the coolest things I ever saw. Murgatroyd, or whoever he was, got away with it, too. Wow!"

"It was awesome," Phil agreed. "And that poetry reading and vomit party were pretty wild. Exciting things are finally happening around this place."

"Yeah, they are," said Natasha. She grinned and, then, brushed her lips softly against his. "It's about time, isn't it?"

# Chapter 29

## The Rebellion Gathers Momentum

After three days of staging dramatic events, the conspirators decided to take a little break, both to refresh their energies and to begin preparing themselves for hijinks at UAardvark's graduation ceremonies that coming weekend.

Nevertheless, on the day after the controversial press conference, as the sun spread its rays over UAardvark, other subversive forces were on the move, this time among students.

Natasha and Phil woke up late that morning, in his bed, with their limbs still partially intertwined. They felt happy and exhilarated, not only by their blossoming relationship, but also by the growing revolt on the campus.

Taped on Phil's wall was a leaflet he had torn off a classroom bulletin board when no one was looking. Produced by the administration during less turbulent times, the leaflet proclaimed: "37% of UAardvark Students Are Planning to Enter the Business World." Writing in magic marker, Phil had added to the sentence: "And Will Be the Worse for It." Right next to the leaflet, he had affixed a newspaper clipping recounting the chaos on Corporate Celebration Day.

"What a blast this place has become," Natasha said. Arising from the bed, she pulled on her jeans and slid her sweater over her head.

"Yeah," Phil remarked. "It's hard to believe. Reality is taking on a whole new, fantastic dimension."

"You know, Phil, it wouldn't be hard to push things even further."

"What do you mean?" he asked.

"Phil, you're really good at computer-type technical stuff, right?"

"Sure," he said. "I've been working on it with Benjamin Hughes."

"Well, do you think you can lift the administration's promotional videos off the university website and, then, change the sound track?"

Smiling, he replied: "No problem. Why do you want to do that?"

"I was thinking," she said, as a mischievous gleam came into her eyes, "we could substitute donkeys braying, pigs squealing, and turkeys gobbling for the words of administrators."

"That's terrific," he responded, starting to laugh.

"But wait, wait," she added, getting into a laughing jag herself. "Then we broadcast the videos on all the campus television sets! Can that be arranged?"

"Damn right!" he chortled, pulling her down to the bed once more.

"Phil, you're great," she said, with another laugh. "But let's save sex for later. First we're going to take care of those videos."

And that's what they did. By three o'clock, videos of campus administrators—braying, squealing, and gobbling—were being broadcast on the thousands of television sets that saturated the campus. By half past four, virtually the entire student body was sprawled in front of the glowing screens, laughing hysterically.

Belatedly discovering that another catastrophe was

underway, President Hopkins ordered the vice president for campus television to use his central control gadgetry to shut off the entire TV system. But, almost as soon as he did this, it came on again, with either the same video or a new one—this one packed with film footage of the wealthy alumni, covered in vomit.

Meanwhile, recognizing that a high-tech struggle was going on between the administration and mysterious antagonists, students crowded around the TV sets, cheering each time a subversive video returned. The video screenings continued until after dinner, when they suddenly ceased. The reason remained a mystery. In fact, the temporary halt in programming had come about because Natasha and Phil could no longer resist the pull of taking time out for some celebratory sex.

* * *

Later that evening, after a meeting with the conspirators at the Galway, Jake walked back to his house and discovered Ellen sitting on his front porch steps, waiting for him.

"How did I rate this good fortune?" he asked, a bit stiffly, sitting down beside her.

"Well, you know, I've never stopped being concerned about you, Jake," Ellen replied. "And I've even heard rumors that you've stopped drinking."

"Yes, I've heard that, too," he said, still hurt by her recent dismissal of his romantic interest, but heartened by this renewed contact.

"Anyway, I wanted you to know that I'm really pleased about that, Jake. And you're looking better, too."

"Well, like the fine wines I no longer drink, I guess I get better with age."

She laughed, and then paused a moment, finally saying: "Also, I think you might have something to do with all this anti-administration stuff going on around campus."

"Oh, why is that?" Jake asked, as innocently as he could.

"Well, for one thing, you taught English to those Hells Angels types who did the reading on campus the other day. For another, Harry told me."

"Ah, Harry. He greatly magnifies my significance in the scheme of things. And, anyway, I'm not at liberty to talk about it, even to women of whom I'm enamored."

She laughed and waved her hand at him as if he were hopeless.

"But seriously, Ellen, I'm really glad you stopped by. I wanted to speak with you about your own life, but, in the aftermath of our stress-filled parting, I didn't know how to begin."

She looked at him quietly.

"First Frank died," Jake said. "And then those bastards in the administration fired you. I can't begin to tell you how sorry I am." He paused. "Are you starting to look for other jobs?"

"Oh yes, I am," she said with a sad smile. "But it's hard to do it. Since Frank's death, I've been feeling pretty listless, unable to do much of anything. Also, I think it's very unlikely that I'll be hired anywhere. After all, any potential new bosses will just contact the old ones. And you can imagine what the old ones will say about me."

"Well, don't despair. Who knows how long Hopkins and his court will last around this place?" Jake remarked, with a grin. "He does seem to be encountering some unusual difficulties, doesn't he?"

\* \* \*

Even as Ellen and Jake discussed President Hopkins, he was engaged in an intense telephone conversation with J. Edgar Beria, the director of the Federal Bureau of Inquisitions.

"How's your investigation of these campus incidents coming along, J. Edgar?" asked the university president.

"Not well, Dwight. Not well at all," remarked the FBI chieftain. "We began with efforts to infiltrate Aardvark's Muslim mosque. But my agents discovered that there is none! Then we tried to speak with local Muslims. But there aren't any! Of course, there used to be some on your campus. But that was before the Immigration Bureau began denying visas to people who were suspiciously Muslim."

"Do you think you could ease the restrictions?" asked the university president. "Then maybe there'd be some Muslims around here who could be investigated."

"We've thought of that, Dwight. But, unfortunately, Muslims don't seem to want to come to the United States any more, no matter what we do."

"Well, that's a sad state of affairs, J. Edgar."

"But I want you to know that we're not giving up, Dwight. I've dispatched 10 of my top agents to Japan to investigate those haiku."

"And how are they doing?"

"Well, they're having trouble, for they don't speak Japanese—or whatever those funny-looking little people speak over there. According to my agents' latest reports, some of them are now lost in the Tokyo subways. So we're off to a slow start."

"OK, just keep me informed, J. Edgar. We've got to get to the bottom of this!"

# Chapter 30

## Graduation Day

Graduation day at UAardvark was scheduled for late April, about two weeks earlier than in the past and on most other college and university campuses. The administration had decided that, as the content of courses didn't matter very much, the academic year should be shortened. This would have the benefit of reducing labor costs, as the faculty would be paid proportionately less. It would also free campus facilities for well-funded corporate "retreats," during which managerial employees would be encouraged—in newly-constructed spa facilities utilizing mud baths, shiatsu massages, and a variety of gentle games—to find "inner peace."

Although the conspirators had worked out a plan to liven up graduation day at UAardvark, they realized that it presented them with some new and serious obstacles. To carry it off successfully, they would have to line up a substantial portion of the faculty, thereby endangering whatever anonymity they still retained. Also, they were unsure how students and, especially, parents, would react to a little creative disruption. Even so, the conspirators felt it was worth a try, particularly because graduation day provided one of the few times when so many members of the university community gathered together. Also, of course, the event would be well covered by the mass media.

For a time, everything went as scheduled. Amid traditional graduation music piped into the vast Cutter Insect Repellent Auditorium, where parents were already seated, faculty members, administrators, and students filed into the room in their colorful academic robes. The faculty and administrators sat in chairs on a stage, facing the students, their parents, and their guests.

After some welcoming remarks, President Hopkins, looking bleary eyed and a bit worse for wear thanks to recent events, introduced the featured speaker: General Helmut B. Warthog. General Warthog, he explained, was a former planner of the successful U.S. invasion of Jamaica ("at a time when that nation threatened the very survival of the Free World") and, subsequently, chair of the Joint Chiefs of Staff. Currently, the president said, General Warthog chaired the board of the General Weapons Corporation, one of the nation's leading defense contractors.

Polite applause followed from most of those present. But the clapping was particularly long and loud from the ranks of the faculty, thus lengthening it for at least five minutes. Surprised and pleased by the prolonged ovation, President Hopkins considered it a good omen.

Launching into his address ("The Academic-Military-Industrial Partnership"), General Warthog got no further than his first two sentences before another burst of applause from the faculty led to a very lengthy ovation from the audience. Looking bewildered, the general stopped for a moment and, then, resumed his remarks.

As he spoke fondly of the need to increase production by restoring the nation's work ethic, a faculty member suddenly yelled out: "Yes, yes. Restore flogging!" Once again, the faculty burst into applause, triggering clapping elsewhere in the room.

Beginning to sense that something was wrong, General Warthog turned to foreign affairs, explaining that Americans lived in a dangerous world of international competition, even with friendly nations. "Bomb them, bomb them!" hollered faculty members, many of whom now whipped out American flags from under their academic robes and began to wave them. More applause followed, amid murmuring that grew throughout the hall. Taking a gulp of air, the general plunged forward with his talk.

"Also, of course," he said, "there are our many enemies." In response, faculty—their flags now waving furiously—chanted: "Crucify them, crucify them!"

Even Hopkins now recognized that something was wrong, although he wasn't quite sure what to do about it. After all, there was nothing improper about applauding, cheering, or waving the American flag. And the sentiments expressed struck him as appropriately patriotic.

The students, though, got the drift of things, and now began to join in the fun. When General Warthog made a derisive joke about pot-smoking students, several of the more rambunctious students in the audience shouted out: "Hang them, hang them!" On stage, faculty applauded and waved their flags, many of which were embossed with corporate logos. A growing portion of the audience laughed and clapped with glee.

In a desperate attempt to save the situation, the general put a brittle smile on his face and declared: "Of course, I'm one of the new breed of executives. We all understand that the modern corporation, like the armed forces, enables you to savor life and relax with your friends. Why not have a little fun?"

A yelp promptly went up from several dozen students, who took off their clothes and began to dance in the aisles. Meanwhile, faculty members applauded vigorously and yelled out their support. Some joined the crowd of student dancers, which was rapidly growing larger.

Recognizing that he had lost control of the situation, General Warthog pressed the red button on his security pager, whereupon six burly corporate security guards burst through a side door and onto the stage. They surrounded him and, pushing aside administrators and faculty members, barreled forward toward the nearest exit. As numerous students and parents were in the way, the security guards slammed into them, sending them reeling back into other attendees or falling to the floor. One mother who had idolized the general for years got close enough to him to hold out her autograph book. But General Warthog, convinced that she was mocking him, straight-armed her in the chest, thereby shoving the astonished woman into the pile of students and parents. Then, within moments, the angry general and his retinue were out the door, in his limousine, and speeding away to the Aardvark Airport.

Aghast at the situation, President Hopkins managed to reach the microphone and, then, announce to the noisy gathering that, given these disturbing developments, graduation was being postponed. This immediately inspired a wave of booing and hooting from the audience, most of which was now on its feet. Students and parents, after all, assumed that they had reached the culmination of a long, hard, expensive slog through UAardvark. And some, at least, had rather enjoyed the confrontation with General Warthog.

But, within minutes, most abandoned the auditorium and stood about, outside, discussing the startling event among themselves and with reporters, who were all keyed up to file new and juicy stories on another day's mischief at UAardvark.

The faculty departed more quickly, reluctant to be grilled by administrators about their overenthusiastic embrace of General Warthog. As Jake and his poker crew said their goodbyes outside the auditorium building before heading home, they raised their thumbs in a sign of another day's success.

Meanwhile, standing not far away, a group of tall, well-built men in dark raincoats and slouch hats eyed departing faculty members intently and followed them to the parking lots. There they copied down the license plate numbers of faculty cars.

About a half hour later, in the now largely deserted auditorium, Hopkins and his vice presidents assessed the damage, which they concluded had been substantial. After all, a key figure from the military-industrial complex had stormed out in a rage, parents blamed the administration for the mess, students were growing ever more rebellious, and faculty members were clearly getting out of hand.

"I would have fired those eggheads on the spot if I hadn't already arranged to get rid of them by eliminating the liberal arts departments," Hopkins remarked. "Maybe I should rehire them so that I can appropriately punish them. What do you think, Watkins?" he asked the vice president for vice presidents.

"It's Jones, Mr. President," replied the vice president for vice presidents. "And I don't think it's worth rehiring them. Too much paperwork. Anyway, it's not entirely clear who our enemies are anymore."

"That's true, Jones," President Hopkins said. "I was tempted to call in the campus security police. But, with all that's going on around here these days, I'm not even sure of their loyalty."

"Well, you can count on our loyalty, Mr. President," said the ever-ingratiating vice president for plumbing. "And, anyway, what else can they possibly do to us?"

# Chapter 31

# The New Technology Center Exposed

On the day after the ill-fated graduation ceremony, the conspirators held another press conference at the Strand. This one, however, was not a put-on. In fact, it was a deadly serious event, for Jake and Helen were set to reveal the administration's plan for storing nuclear waste in the New Technology Center.

Even before beginning, they realized that they faced two major problems.

The first was that, to avoid implicating Marsha, they were not going to reveal the source of their information. And this was bound to undermine its credibility.

The second problem was that virtually all the television, radio, and press representatives in attendance worked for the giant communications media, which were corporations. Yes, these journalists had been happy, in recent days, to file reports on hijinks at UAardvark. But this new story was going to be much less palatable, for it involved exposing a very nasty corporate project. Even if the media representatives personally sympathized with Jake and Helen, they would realize that the story would probably receive a chilly response from their bosses.

Also, of course, Jake and Helen were risking their jobs by playing a public role in this event. But, at the moment, the two of them, facing a roomful of sharp-toothed media sharks, regarded that as the least of their worries.

Opening the press conference, Jake announced that representatives of the media had been invited to attend because he and other concerned faculty members at UAardvark had important information to disclose to them and to the general public.

Helen then circulated among the attendees and distributed copies of the documents that Marsha had secretly photocopied. As the media representatives pored over these materials, an excited buzz enveloped the room.

Finally, as cameras whirred and lights flashed, Jake briefly outlined what the documents revealed. "It comes down to an arrangement to secretly store large quantities of highly radioactive nuclear waste, including body parts and other nuclear debris, right in the middle of the UAardvark campus," he said. "There is no educational reason or justification for this venture. It is a purely financial measure, in which a university sells itself for large amounts of corporate cash."

Helen followed, remarking: "We all know, or certainly should, just how harmful these kinds of radioactive materials are, and how they will destroy the health and lives of many people on this campus. Despite this fact—indeed, probably because of it—there are no apparent plans to submit this shocking deal to the students, faculty, and staff of the university for their consideration or comment."

Just as Jake and Helen had feared, the media representatives threw tough, sometimes hostile, questions at them.

A burly man from Fox News aggressively demanded: "How do you know these documents aren't fabricated?"

In response, Jake pointed out that they had received the materials from a very credible source and, furthermore, that the stationery and the signatures matched those of the executive officers of CCInc and UAardvark. "Also," he said, "if you have any doubts about authenticity, why don't you ask William Swagger V and Dwight Hopkins about the documents, and also whether they have agreed to this nuclear waste-dumping scheme?"

Another journalist, this one from CNN, asked: "Isn't it possible that this plan is just preliminary, and that it won't ultimately be implemented?"

Helen replied: "I suggest that you ask Swagger and Hopkins about that."

"But aren't you assuming that nuclear waste is harmful?" a well-dressed reporter for *Business Week* inquired.

For a moment, Jake was flabbergasted, but then replied: "Yes!"

Despite themselves, the journalists erupted in laughter.

In the aftermath of the conference, Helen was interviewed by a slick, brittle-looking woman with dyed-blond hair from Fox News, who—after her makeup had been carefully applied by her handlers—proceeded to inquire about how the campus exposé was connected to the liberal War on Religion.

Jake consented to an interview with a scruffy young man from the leftwing Freedom Now radio program, who pressed him on links between the Hopkins administration and the 9/11 attacks.

Other journalists took Jake and Helen's advice by phoning Swagger and Hopkins.

* * *

When the first calls from the reporters started coming in, Swagger cursed to himself and briefly stopped checking his net worth. Then he met with his public relations staff. Ultimately, they distributed an official statement saying that CCInc was not in the habit of revealing its private business arrangements.

With that disposed of, Swagger brooded on what could have gone wrong. That idiot Hopkins must have screwed up, he thought. But it also occurred to him that the leak might have come from his own headquarters. Accordingly, he buzzed his vice president for internal security and ordered an immediate investigation of his staff.

President Hopkins was at least as disturbed when the journalists started to phone him. Those troublemakers, Jake Holland and Helen Meyerson, would certainly have to be fired—at least once the media packed up and went home. But, more seriously, he thought, as he rolled his new miniature racing car across his desk, how could this have happened? He, too, suspected that the leak had developed elsewhere—in this case, with Swagger and CCInc. But, of course, it remained possible that the traitor was located on his own campus. Phoning Marsha, he told her to arrange for the vice president for surveillance to contact him immediately.

Marsha did so, breathing a sigh of relief. That vice president, she knew, was perhaps the most incompetent of the lot. She also phoned Helen to tell her what was happening in the president's office and to compliment her on her performance.

Meanwhile, Hopkins sat down with his public relations staff, and, together, they drafted a short statement for the media. "Due to the sensitive nature of this issue, which touches on high-level national security matters," declared the statement, "we are unable to confirm or deny these reckless allegations."

\* \* \*

That evening, when the revelations about the New Technology Center were aired on the national television networks, the stories were cautiously constructed and muted. Moreover, the statements by Swagger and Hopkins were quoted in full, thus giving them more airtime than the revelations.

Nor did the mass media's reluctance to challenge corporate arrangements provide the only indication that the campus rebels faced an uphill struggle. During the press conference, Jake had noticed a contingent of tall, well-built men in raincoats sitting in the audience. And when he left the hotel to return home, two of them followed him to his car. Deciding that confrontation was the best policy in the circumstances, he turned around abruptly and demanded: "Who the hell are you? And why are you following me?"

"Take it easy, Jake," the bigger of them said, standing his ground. "We're only doing our job."

"And what's that?" asked Jake.

In answer, the second of his pursuers took out his wallet and held up his identification: FBI. Smiling unpleasantly, he said: "Anything you want to tell us about what's going on around here, Jake? We sure hope you're not causing all that trouble on campus."

"Now why would I want to do that?" Jake asked. Then, after a short staring contest, he got in his car and drove toward his home. En route, he mumbled to himself: "Well, well, the feds are out in force. I guess some folks are getting nervous."

# Chapter 32

# The Investigation

J. Edgar Beria sat at his desk in the Federal Bureau of Inquisitions Building in downtown Washington, DC, brooding on his fate.

Everyone portrayed him as an unfeeling monster, he thought sadly. But that was a calumny! After all, during his college years, he had dabbled in the arts, and ever since then he had been painting the most delicate of flowers, coached in the process by a demanding inner voice, to which he had attached the name Jeffrey. A sweet boy, Jeffrey bore his first name—the one that his mother had given him before he later discarded it in his public life. Jeffrey intervened sometimes in his FBI career, but his sensitivity was almost invariably overcome by Edgar's insistence upon repression. Edgar, another inner voice, understood that people were dirty and evil, and had to be kept in line. The result of their conflicting demands—J. Edgar's grim persona—was well-known to frightened politicians and to the public. But few knew of the psychological turmoil that underlay it, symbolized by the many paintings of flowers, as well as the many awards for service as FBI director, that adorned his office walls.

"Why am I not happier?" he wondered. Actually, he knew why. It was these damned investigations! Jeffrey was appalled by J. Edgar's poking about in people's private lives, destroying their careers, dragging them off to prison, and (only when useful, of course) torturing them. Jeffrey didn't understand—as Edgar did—the necessity of safeguarding the Free World and seeing to it that American citizens pursued disciplined, orderly existences. Nor did Jeffrey show proper concern about the encroachments upon the FBI's turf by those incompetents in the CIA and in local police forces, the attacks upon him by the jackals in the liberal media, and the lawsuits of the damned civil libertarians. Who could really appreciate J. Edgar's torments and sufferings? A tear trickled down his cheek. "Be brave," he told himself.

Buzzing his secretary, he ordered her to get Dwight Hopkins on the line. Ever since that disastrous press conference the other day, Hopkins had been pestering him for the results of the FBI investigation of the mess at UAardvark.

"You shouldn't be involved in this," Jeffrey told him plaintively.

"Shut up, Jeffrey," said Edgar. "You're out of your depth. Go paint some flowers."

Finally, Hopkins came on the line. "Any news, J. Edgar? You can't imagine the pressure I'm under here, especially after yesterday's publicity about the New Technology Center."

"Well," said J. Edgar, "I certainly sympathize with your difficulties."

"Why? Why should you?" Jeffrey asked J. Edgar.

"Butt out, Butthead," said Edgar.

"J. Edgar, are you there?" asked Hopkins.

"Yes," said a rattled J. Edgar, "I was just thinking about how to formulate things for you. I suppose I should say that, in our investigation of UAardvark, there's some bad news and some good news. The bad news is that we still don't know who, exactly, is responsible for all the troublemaking."

"Why is that?" asked Hopkins.

"Well," said J. Edgar, "it boils down to the fact that, although we have a wealth of information, it's very unreliable. For example, my agents have done extensive interviews with the faculty participants in that chaotic graduation ceremony. And it turns out that they all blame different people, often pointing to ancient quarrels with members of their departments. It was such a snake pit of personal feuds and petty grievances that the interviews went on at great length and gave my agents terrible headaches. Four of them, in fact, up and quit the agency! What kind of faculty do you have there, Dwight?"

"Oh, they're terrible people, all right," Hopkins said. "And I'm in the process of getting rid of them. But what else have you done?"

J. Edgar gave a sigh, and then said: "A key part of our investigation was checking out the records at your campus library, to see what students are reading. And what we found was that students never borrow any books. Instead, they borrow DVDs. Over the past year, the only really suspicious DVDs they signed out were films by the Marx Brothers. Well, that name rang a bell, you can bet! And so we watched a lot of those films before some young wise guy in the agency figured out that the commie Marx wasn't one of the brothers—although for a while we thought he might be Harpo.

"Of course," J. Edgar continued, "there were some particularly difficult aspects to this investigation. Our agents in the dorms frequently became intoxicated by marijuana fumes, and I am sad to say that a few bad apples among them enjoyed it so much that they 'went rogue.'"

"No!" cried Hopkins, feigning surprise.

"Oh yes. And something similar happened to our agent infiltrating the Hells Angels. Although he succeeded in working his way into that group, he enjoyed riding motorcycles and, especially, writing poetry so much that, in the words of his supervisor, he 'went native.'"

"How can you blame him?" asked Jeffrey. "Who hasn't wanted to write poetry?"

"Good agents don't write poetry, you *$&%(^," Edgar snarled.

Shaking off his inner demons, J. Edgar concluded: "I should also mention that the investigation was made much more complicated thanks to competing investigations by other government agencies and private entities. In fact, many of the investigative reports by our agents turned out to provide information on other agents. This multitude of material was then fed into the FBI's new computers, which suffered a breakdown from data overload—although, as we later learned, some of the computer difficulties were caused by many of our agents simultaneously using the computers to play video games."

"But J. Edgar," said Hopkins, "I thought you said that there is also some good news."

"You're right, Dwight, there is. One of your vice presidents—um, the vice president for vending machines—recently came to our attention as the only member of the university administration who seems to work on campus from nine to five, five days a week. This immediately led us to grow suspicious, and our suspicions were confirmed when, after we placed him under drone surveillance and thoroughly searched his home, we found nothing incriminating."

"Excuse me, J. Edgar, but if you found nothing incriminating, why did this confirm your suspicions?"

"Well, you're not in the law enforcement business, Dwight. And so you don't understand the evil that lurks everywhere. In fact, everyone is involved in some transgression of the law or propriety. Therefore, when nothing can be found along these lines, it's obvious that it's being deliberately concealed. And that sends up a red flag to those of us guarding the ramparts of national security."

"I see," said Hopkins.

"Anyway," J. Edgar continued, "we've whisked him off to one of the nation's overseas 'black sites' for special interrogation. Although he has not confessed to anything yet, we realize that this is just one more sign of his guilt."

"But what about Jake Holland and Helen Meyerson?" inquired Hopkins, now a bit impatient. "They showed their subversive hands pretty clearly the other day, didn't they?"

"Yes, of course they did," said J. Edgar. "But, alas, for the time being, we can't touch them. After all, they've become public figures, and their arrest would be controversial. Meanwhile, rest assured, we're investigating them and finding all sorts of juicy information. Holland, for example, is a Jew. So you can be pretty sure he's up to no good. And this Meyerson woman, we've discovered, is a lesbian, and belongs to a 'women's group.' Our drone hovering outside the window of one of her group's meetings reported an intense discussion of 'agenda stereotypes,' and we're now running this item through one of our repaired computers to figure out what it means. So don't worry, Dwight. We're onto them—and onto your vice president, who we assume will confess soon. It's just a matter of time before we crush them all."

In the background, Jeffrey groaned while Edgar laughed.

With the conversation completed, J. Edgar put down the phone and stared bleakly at his paintings of flowers. No, the nation didn't appreciate his sacrifices. Another tear trickled down his cheek.

# Chapter 33

## The General Strike

Later on that same morning, Jake and Sam sat in their respective offices, conferring by phone. Sam complimented Jake once again on how he had handled the press conference. But Jake brushed his praise aside, saying that the real credit for exposing the New Technology Center should go to Marsha and Helen, without whom they never would have secured the incriminating documents.

"How about clueing me in on what's going to happen today on campus?" said Jake.

Sam just laughed. "Well, the cleaning and maintenance workers are planning something. But I'll be damned if I know what it is!"

Suddenly, though, as they were speaking, the lights in their offices went off. Indeed, the lights and computers in offices and classrooms all across the campus died abruptly, a clear indication that the electricity had stopped flowing. Gradually, bewildered faculty, students, administrators, secretaries, and other university personnel began congregating outside their buildings, discussing the mysterious halt to the electric power supply.

Soon after they began gathering, reports reached them that the campus water system had ceased to function, rendering campus toilets and sinks dysfunctional. Lacking electricity, the campus air conditioning had also shut down, leading the many offices, classrooms, and other buildings with sealed windows to become unbearably hot and stuffy.

Frantic lower-level administrative officials tried contacting President Hopkins and his leading vice presidents, but no one could locate them. Finally, a secretary remembered that they were holding a top-level strategy meeting in the rejuvenatron. But, with the electricity no longer functioning, Hopkins and his retinue of vice presidents were trapped in it, unable to get out.

Newspaper and television reporters, alerted to yet another crisis on the UAardvark campus, streamed onto its grounds. Yet, despite their best efforts, they remained just as confused as the rest of the milling crowd about what was going on and why.

Then, suddenly, out of the Tunnels, surged hundreds of campus cleaning and maintenance workers, wearing their working grays supplemented by red armbands. Chanting slogans and marching forward, they held aloft large banners reading "STRIKE!" and "Let's Dump the Bosses off Our Backs!" They distributed leaflets to the wide-eyed crowd, urging everyone to gather on the university's great lawn. Renamed Commerce Plaza by the Hopkins administration, it was referred to by the workers and their leaflets as Social Justice Plaza.

As several thousand members of the campus community gathered at the plaza, a Workers Chorus, amplified by microphones, belted out "Solidarity Forever," giving particular emphasis to the line: "Without our brain and muscle, not a single wheel can turn."

At the end of the song, Tom Rowley—his dark skin aglow in the warm sunshine—took the microphone and bellowed out: "Welcome, brothers and sisters. We have seized the moment, and our class enemies are on the run!"

A roar of approval went up from the crowd. Looking around

at the many faculty members, students, and others who, only weeks before, had seemed the epitome of apathy, Jake could hardly believe it. Had he underestimated them? Had he missed a hidden element of disgust with commercial domination that, with some encouragement, had finally erupted into action? But he broke off his musings, for the immediate reality was too good to miss. With a shiver of delight, Jake turned his attention back to the charismatic cleaning worker at the microphone, now winding up his brief peroration.

"Our class enemies, as you know, are the corporate plunderers who have no respect for you or for education," Tom was saying, as the sweat rolled down his face. "Their only concerns are building their empires and maximizing their profits. They think they are the masters of the universe. But they are wrong. For, ultimately, the people are more powerful than all their hoarded wealth. It is time to rise up against their rule—their *mis*rule—and create decent lives for ourselves, for our families, and for all of humankind!"

Another roar came from the crowd, now beginning to feel its power.

Replacing Tom at the microphone, Eva said: "Brothers and sisters, comrades in the struggle. Are you with us?"

Another roar.

"Good!" she shouted. "Because today we are proclaiming a strike, not by the cleaning and maintenance workers alone, but by everyone who supports social and economic justice. It is a general strike, which requires all of us to cease working or studying on this campus until our demands are met. And what are our demands? Only two. First, the ouster of the administration!"

The crowd went wild, and it took several minutes before Eva could continue.

"And second," she said, "the establishment of a new regime, run by the workers and the students on this campus!"

Pandemonium ensued, driven by disdain for the administration and the audacity of the proposals. Although the president and vice president of UUF were nowhere to be seen, other leaders of the faculty union (including some who had never dared say a word against the administration) spoke up to pledge UUF's support for the general strike. Natasha, the heroine of the student body after the daring screening of her anti-administration videos, brought the crowd to its feet by proclaiming that any students who had any guts would rise up in solidarity.

The campus police, who had just arrived after finally managing to free the top campus administrators from the rejuvenatron, were so swept up in the fervor that they, too, pledged their support for the general strike. Indeed, a contingent of the most zealous police promptly raced back to the anteroom of the rejuvenatron, located President Hopkins and his vice presidents drying themselves off there, and shoved them back into the gadget.

Jake and Sam, observing the scene, were ecstatic.

Jake said: "I can't believe this is happening, Sam. I know you've been talking with these workers, especially the ones in the Tunnels. But we didn't plan this. What's going on? Why are they joining us?"

"You really don't know?" asked Sam. "With all your reading of Jack London, you still don't get it?"

"No, Sam. Not really. What's happening?"

"It's the class struggle, Jake. Right here on this campus. It's the rebirth of the #@$#(*&^+ wonderful class struggle!"

# Chapter 34

# The UAardvark Spring

As the rebellion grew on the UAardvark campus, news about it began to spread to other colleges and universities across the nation. In part, this was because reports on events at UAardvark were carried by the mass media—although often in a very sensational and distorted form. But it also resulted from the fact that students, faculty, and other workers at different educational institutions used e-mail, telephones, and social media to share reports on what was happening with their own friends and networks. Many recognized similarities between the corporatization of UAardvark and developments on their own campuses and, therefore, found the growing revolt against it both relevant and exciting.

Public colleges and universities had been particularly hard hit by the corporate takeover of educational institutions and government. Although these schools were originally established to provide free, high-quality higher education for all, severe cutbacks in public funding had led to larger classes, fewer faculty and staff, and deteriorating facilities. Furthermore, huge tuition increases were making higher education unaffordable for everyone but the wealthy. In addition, their students were engulfed in a tsunami of corporate propaganda, their course offerings and faculty were "restructured" or eliminated to create business-friendly environments, and their blue-collar workers were exploited to the fullest possible extent.

Private colleges and universities shared some of these

features. And yet, there were also some differences. At the most prestigious, expensive institutions, the administrators were brighter and smoother. They didn't dare to cut liberal arts courses (as the wealthy expected their children to be introduced to world culture and civilization), never thought of eliminating foreign language programs (as the wealthy expected their children to travel abroad and, ultimately, to manage multinational corporations), and avoided subjecting their students to everyday corporate propaganda (as it was too crass). Even so, the deference of such institutions to the wealthy and powerful, their establishment of Free Enterprise chairs, and their close relations with major banking and corporate interests were well known to—and often resented by—members of the campus community.

Thus, as protest campaigns erupted at UAardvark, they burst forth elsewhere, as well. At the City College of New York, students ripped down the corporate logos. At the University of Wisconsin, the faculty went on strike, demanding union recognition. At San Francisco State College, the maintenance workers walked off the job. At Texas Tech, students tore down the corporate names on buildings and spray-painted them with new, more appropriate ones. At Southern Illinois University, the cafeteria workers staged a sit-down strike. At Columbia University, the faculty voted "no confidence" in the administration. At the University of Montana, students destroyed the ubiquitous television sets. At the University of South Carolina, striking janitorial workers set up a "Hooverville" at the campus gates. Throughout the state of Michigan, students organized a boycott of classes, which they said would continue until tuition was lowered by 50 percent.

Commenting on the growing revolt sweeping American campuses, some observers began to talk of a UAardvark Spring.

Others took a more dire view of events. Fox News pounded away at the thesis that the remaining Democrats in Congress were responsible for "the campus riots" that "threatened America's very survival."

David Horowitz, the self-anointed expert on American colleges and universities, explained on its broadcasts that "sixties rejects, perverts, rapists, drug addicts, Communists, terrorists, feminists, and other anti-Americans" had instigated the campus protests in order to turn the United States into an Islamic republic.

Similarly, on the far Left, some elements also were wary of the UAardvark Spring. Issuing a statement on behalf of its 27 members, the League of Revolutionary Workers and Peasants declared that the campus activists were "objectively" counterrevolutionary, for their rebellion had failed to mobilize the masses against U.S. imperialism.

Emphasizing the political errors of this line of thought, the League of Revolutionary Peasants and Workers—which had split off from the League of Revolutionary Workers and Peasants six months before—promptly responded that the UAardvark uprising *did* have the potential for mobilizing the masses, but only if it adopted the League's 19-point program.

Mainstream politicians also weighed in on the issue. The Republican Party's presidential candidate called for an immediate, full-scale U.S. military attack on American college and university campuses, followed by a U.S. military occupation of indefinite duration. "Setting a date for withdrawal would only encourage our enemies," he said.

By contrast, the Democratic presidential candidate argued that economic sanctions should be given a chance to work before the president ordered a U.S. Army, Navy, and Air Force assault. Meanwhile, he said, the U.S. military budget should, of course, be increased.

Polls of public opinion showed that 1 percent of Americans favored a military attack, 2 percent favored sanctions, 42 percent favored no action, and 55 percent hadn't heard of the issue.

Naturally, the National Association of College and University Trustees was aghast at the situation. But it remained unsure of how to deal with it. On the one hand, it didn't want its multibillion-dollar educational facilities destroyed in a military attack. On the other, it certainly didn't want them managed by faculty, students, and a bunch of scruffy blue-collar workers. As a result, it announced that it was commissioning a study of the issue by University Management, Inc.—one of the educational branches of CCInc.

Of course, CCInc's president, William T. Swagger V, didn't need any prompting to make his views known to Dwight Hopkins. Getting the UAardvark president on the phone, he launched into a string of profanities. Then, calming down a bit, he roared: "What the ^)*%(& do you think you're doing there, Hopkins? All hell is breaking loose on your campus and, as a result, around the nation! Business confidence is being shaken! The value of my investments has declined to"—here he glanced at his iPad—"\$6.21 billion. This is unconscionable!"

"I understand, Swagger, I understand," Hopkins said nervously. "But I'm doing my best."

"Well your best isn't good enough, you dumb *&)^)*&^! How did our agreement on the New Technology Center get out there in public? That was supposed to be top secret."

"I kept it secret, Swagger. I really did. But, somehow, we were discovered. Are you sure that it wasn't revealed from your end of operations?"

"You *&()^)^%+! I run a tight ship here!" Swagger stormed. "And, anyway, I've ordered a full internal security investigation. I've already fired seven people because of it."

"Does that mean you've uncovered the whistleblowers?" Hopkins asked eagerly.

"No. I just thought it would be a good means of keeping people in line."

"Of course, of course," said Hopkins. "I ordered an investigation of my own, but I haven't discovered any weak link yet."

"Well, whether or not you discover someone," Swagger remarked, his anger rising once again, "I expect you to stamp out this rebellion on your campus. This situation can't be allowed to go on any longer! Do you understand that, Hopkins?"

"Yes, of course," Hopkins began, but suddenly realized that Swagger had hung up on him.

Swagger was right, thought Hopkins. But what was he to do? He mused about this for a few minutes and, then, decided to call Wilma. After all, she was the president of the faculty union. She, if anyone, should be able to cool down those faculty hotheads.

Dialing her home number and waiting for her to pick up

the phone, he once more thought of her beautiful, green-tinted skin, her erotic black clothing, that cruel, exciting look on her face. . . . He gripped his model racing car tightly.

"Hello, who is this?" she snapped, warily.

"Wilma, darling," he answered. "It's me, Dwight."

# Chapter 35

## Confusion among the Christian Patriots

In the early evening, shortly after the New Technology Center exposé, several dozen members of the Christian Patriots gathered at the Americanism Defense Fortress for a debriefing and general discussion of the previous week's events. Although the group's surveillance teams had gathered lots of information during their operations, interpreting it was proving difficult. In fact, members of the Christian Patriots were thoroughly befuddled about what was happening at UAardvark. Thus, tonight they looked forward to coming up with a coherent understanding of things.

The evening began near the farm's rotting barn with an impressive color guard ceremony and salute to the flag, presided over by Colonel Bumpkin. Then, with a sigh of relief, the sweating, overweight men sank into their folding chairs, swatted away gathering mosquitoes, and opened up cool bottles of beer.

Sergeant Harris, reporting for the team that had observed Corporate Celebration Day, observed that, although he had never thought much of poetry—"literary stuff," as he put it, "written by queers and pansies"—the poems at the UAardvark event weren't half bad. In fact, he said, he thought "a lot of them expressed good, red-blooded American values. And the men who read them certainly looked like God-fearing patriots." Consequently, he and other team members couldn't understand why so many people left early.

In the ensuing discussion, no one else was able to explain that satisfactorily, either.

The Rev. Billy Ray Jones, the leader of the surveillance team for the alumni luncheon, explained that he and the other Christian Patriots hadn't been in the banquet hall. But, when they saw people fleeing the hall covered with vomit or vomiting outside it, they concluded that something must have been wrong with the food. Having noticed, with apprehension, the advent of Chinese and Mexican restaurants in Aardvark in recent years, the Rev. Jones thought it likely that the problem on campus had resulted from the serving of foreign food.

"Yeah!" hollered several of the Patriots. One of them added: "And some sort o' Indian place, with colored people and strange smells comin' out the door, opened in town only last week." A consensus quickly formed that this probably explained the sickness on campus.

The gathering also worked out the meaning of the two press conferences, one fake and the other real. Colonel Bumpkin quickly spotted the connection. "They're both part of a plot by the liberal Jew media," he explained. Exactly what the plot was, he couldn't say. But, he added, "everyone knows that those newspapers, radio stations, and television networks are controlled by Socialist-Communist Jews."

That made sense to everyone, and a good feeling spread throughout the gathering as attendees concluded that, despite all the complexities, they were finally getting somewhere.

However, the campus-wide airing of the film of administrators braying, squealing, and gobbling threw them off course. What could it mean? "Maybe they were speaking in tongues," suggested one of the lowly privates. That view was relatively comforting, in that it suggested that these university officials were communing with Jesus or other Higher Powers.

But the Rev. Jones suggested a more disturbing interpretation. "Suppose they was talkin' in a foreign language," he said. "Suppose they was plottin' to institute Sharia law or some other Muslim terrorist thing." As much as the Christian Patriots hoped this was not the case, it certainly remained a live possibility.

What happened on graduation day was also confusing. Sergeant Harris couldn't understand the reason for General Warthog's sudden departure. After all, to judge from the lengthy applause and shouts of approval from the audience, there was a lot of enthusiasm for him and for what he had to say. Perhaps, though, the sergeant remarked, the general had been called away suddenly to deal with a national security emergency. That was understandable. The United States was constantly at war with terrorists and all sorts of other people, as it should be. But why, then, had President Hopkins postponed the graduation ceremony? It remained a mystery, and, given the need for secrecy in national security matters, it would remain so.

Again the gathering was plunged into gloom. And Stan Slobodov's report on the general strike called by the cleaning and maintenance workers did nothing to dispel it.

As the supervisor of the workers and the head of the surveillance team observing them, Slobodov had been giving their action a lot of thought. Their pay and their working conditions were quite satisfactory, Slobodov said, so he concluded that a deeper reason for their behavior was that women had been entering the workforce. "Them women's lib types are destroyin' the family and subvertin' the American way of life."

Although there was a lot of support for this view, the Rev. Jones objected. "The Lord has made women His nat'ral instruments for cleaning," he pointed out. "So why shouldn't women be cleanin' those buildin's?" His logic stopped Slobodov dead in his tracks. And for a time the gathering grew silent and more confused than ever.

Suggesting an alternative explanation, Private McNamara, the FBI infiltrator in their ranks, said that a strike sounded Communist to him. But no one—including McNamara—remembered quite what a Communist thought or looked like, though some in the crowd thought they looked like Democrats.

So, in the absence of any certainty on this score, the Patriots dropped the issue and turned to the most perplexing one of all: the meaning of the deal for the New Technology Center.

Here, at least, Colonel Bumpkin could provide guidance. "It looks to me like an arrangement between President Hopkins and the Jew bankers," he said.

"Is Swagger a Jew?" asked the Rev. Jones. "I heared he was the descendant of a fine old Christian slaveholdin' family."

"He must be a Jew," retorted Colonel Bumpkin. "He's the money man, isn't he?"

"But maybe he's a Muslim," someone suggested. "Them Muslims got lots o' that oil money, don't they? Or maybe he jes works for 'em." Many of the Patriots agreed that either of these was a possibility.

During the week, Colonel Bumpkin explained, surveillance

teams had kept a particularly close watch on Dwight Hopkins and on Jake Holland. Hopkins, one team reported, remained an enigma, for he kept late hours in his office and, even after that, often headed off elsewhere rather than return home. Jake, too, was mysterious, for he left his home late every night, although apparently only to go to a bar. Even so, he was suspiciously dark skinned. To the surveillance team, he looked like an Arab. Maybe, they said, he was a Muslim!

Deciding that the time had come to pull things together, Colonel Bumpkin stood up before the gathering and gave his closing pep talk. "Men, you've done a real heroic job of uncoverin' subversive activities at UAardvark. Unfortunately, though, because of the devious nature of the enemy, we still don't know what it all means. Maybe it means that, as the Good Lord has promised, we are approaching the End Times."

His audience stirred with delight at this, imagining the heathen and other sinners consumed by blood and fire, while they, the righteous, God-fearing patriots, rose to glory.

"Maybe, though," he added, "we are on the verge of an attempted Muslim takeover of our Christian nation."

The Patriots gripped their beer bottles more tightly, steeling themselves for the crucial tasks that lay ahead.

"In either case," said Colonel Bumpkin, "the time has come for us to step up our efforts. We will institute an armed patrol of the UAardvark campus!"

At this command, the gathering was swept by enormous excitement. All of their patriotic zeal, their weapons training, and their knowledge of the enemy were finally coming into play. At last!

With that, the colonel saluted them, and they saluted him in return—a patriotic process they repeated for the next 15 minutes. Then they folded their chairs, packed up their cooler chests, loaded everything in their vans, and drove home to the boredom of their families.

# Chapter 36

## What Next?

Ironically, the UAardvark rebels were also confused—in their case, about their next moves.

Of course, they had been wildly successful so far. Indeed, they had become the cutting edge of a nationwide movement.

Things had certainly changed dramatically on the UAardvark campus. Thanks to the general strike and to the widespread discrediting of the administration, campus governance had fallen into the hands of a Workers and Students Council comprised of student, faculty, professional staff, police, and blue-collar worker representatives. The Council didn't do much governing, though. Nor did it need to, as campus affairs moved along on a voluntary basis in an easygoing, mellow fashion.

During the day, students, faculty, cleaning and maintenance workers, dining-halls workers, police, and others lolled about on the campus lawns, listening to speakers from their ranks. The cleaning and maintenance crews, as well as the professional staff, discussed their backgrounds, the details of their work, and their miserable wages. The faculty adapted their talks to showcase what interested them about their disciplines and to elucidate the roadblocks to intellectual life posed by the corporatization of the university. Students discussed what they wanted in life and what stood in their way of achieving it. The dining-halls workers discussed food nutrition and the filthy conditions in the campus kitchens. And the campus police talked about the difficulties they faced in separating the enforcement of public safety from unnecessarily repressive practices.

As the dining halls were shut down by the strike, a strikers' food committee was organized to obtain food from local farmers and to work at preparing meals for a modest price. Other activists purchased seed and seedlings from the farmers and, then, began cultivating crops on the large university lawns. After dinner, knots of people gathered on different parts of the campus to sing, play instruments, dance, perform plays, and attend poetry readings by The Crusher and the Daffodil Poetry Club. Now that the campus police mingled on a friendly basis with everyone else, the crime rate on campus dropped significantly—although the press pointed out that this resulted, in part, from the unwillingness of police to arrest students who were smoking pot.

Although, in the interest of public health, the maintenance workers agreed to restore the water supply, they continued the electricity shutdown, which had a major impact. The ubiquitous television sets fell silent, as did radios, computers, and assorted sound systems. With more time on their hands, students turned to a variety of other activities, including thinking and even reading books. Lacking lights at night in the dorms and on campus pathways, they adapted to the darkness by engaging in amorous activities throughout the dorms and on the lawns.

In general, the campus revolutionaries were quite pleased with these developments and with the overall sense of excitement that swept through the campus. Even so, they were well aware that the campus administrators still refused to step down from power and continued to occupy their suites of offices.

Although most members of the campus community ignored these university officials, a small portion of the faculty were administration loyalists, apparently because they remained under the sway of Wilma, the witch-like leader of UUF. Worse yet, the continued presence of President Hopkins and his top aides in the official seats of power symbolized the possibility of a return to the old order—the Ancien Régime that had plunged the campus into full-scale commercialization and might still move forward with plans for the New Technology Center and other horrors.

Thus, in a special meeting that night at the Galway, the poker conspirators—joined not only by Ellen but also by members of the Workers and Students Council—expressed their view that the time had come to complete the job of liberating the campus.

But how? The administration stubbornly refused to budge, and behind Hopkins and other administrators stood the board of trustees, the governor, and powerful corporations. As might be expected, these forces were not especially bothered by the existence of plans for a nuclear waste dump on campus. Meanwhile, FBI agents were everywhere and might, someday, actually discover what was happening.

All evening, discussion raged as to the best course of action.

"We have them on the ropes," Helen said, heatedly. "It's time to deliver the knockout blow. Let's seize the state capitol!"

Sam was less enthusiastic about that tactic. "The real power behind this throne is corporate," he said. "What good will challenging elected officials do? It will only lead to a multitude of arrests and lengthy legal entanglements."

Natasha, now quite comfortable with political debates, cut

in at this point. "Students all over the country are fed up with the crap they've been fed by administrators and reactionary politicians," she argued. "We could call for a student strike that would shut down campuses from coast to coast. Then let them try to ignore us!"

Tom countered, though, that students would be ignored if other portions of the campus community were not participants. "You need support from the campus workforce," he said. "And, unfortunately, all too many workers in this country are blinded by false consciousness."

Although the rebels were tantalizingly close to victory, it seemed that they had reached an impasse, with no clear way forward. Some were growing irritated with one another. Others just felt themselves going brain dead from the lengthy discussions.

As the squabbling over strategy continued, Wild Bill Kelly, the owner of the Galway, interrupted their discussion to announce that a woman had phoned and left a message for Jake to call her back.

"Who is it, Bill?" Jake asked.

"Some lady named Mary Jo Hopkins," he replied.

The room was suddenly reduced to silence, broken by Harry: "Jesus, Jake. You run in the fast lane. That's the wife of our beloved university president!"

The room immediately buzzed with conversation. What, the activists wondered, was this all about?

Turning to Harry, Jake said, laughing: "Well, you know I've always been tight with the power elite." Then, after hoots from the crowd, he added: "Hand me your cell phone, Harry. I don't know the woman, but I'm willing to give her a call."

As he did, the room grew silent again, with everyone listening, as best they could, to his conversation.

"Ms. Hopkins?" he said. "This is Jake Holland, returning your phone call." A pause followed, broken by: "Well, sure. If you really want me to." Then there was another pause, after which Jake said: "OK, that's what I'll do."

Turning to the crowd, he grinned. "I thought at first it might be a gag," he said. "But now I don't think so. At least she seems to be the real Ms. Hopkins. And she says that she has something very important to tell me. Right away. At her house."

As pandemonium erupted, Jake winked at the gathering, grabbed his jacket, and hustled out the door.

# Chapter 37

## The Bombshell

Ten minutes later, Jake arrived at the home of Dwight and Mary Jo Hopkins, a university-owned mansion a few blocks from campus. Mary Jo answered his knock on the door and, looking slender and beautiful, admitted him to an ornate hallway.

"Hi," he said, "I'm Jake Holland, a professor of English at the university."

"Hello," she replied, shaking hands with him. "I'm Mary Jo Hopkins. Before we go any further, how about our trying this? You call me Mary Jo and I'll call you Jake."

"Fine," he said smiling. As they headed toward the living room, he asked, as casually as possible: "Will President Hopkins be joining us?"

"No," she said coolly. "He's out. He's often out in the evening." Then, after a pause, she asked: "Can I get you something to drink?"

"Well, coffee, if you don't mind."

While Mary Jo clattered about the kitchen, Jake glanced around the living room. On the walls were numerous pictures of Dwight Hopkins—with his fraternity brothers, with the Yale Young Republicans, with assorted businessmen, and with leading Republican officeholders. He also noticed plenty of miniature racing cars on the coffee table and on bookshelves. At first, Mary Jo's presence was less evident. But, then, spotting books on art, literature, and Eastern philosophy, Jake figured that these must belong to her. Expensive, elegant furniture filled the room.

When Mary Jo returned, carrying a small pot of coffee and cups for both of them, they took seats and chatted amiably for a time. Jake discussed the courses he taught, while Mary Jo asked intelligent questions about them and mentioned, in passing, that she had majored in English at Wellesley.

Impressed, Jake asked her if she had ever considered pursuing a career connected to literature. She replied that she had done so briefly, and had even attended graduate school with that goal in mind. But then Dwight Hopkins came along. He was a handsome, wealthy man who had graduated from one of the nation's finest universities—what her family considered a "good catch." So she had married him and, thanks to the geographical relocations necessitated by his career, dropped out of school. Thereafter, she said, looking down in embarrassment, she had become a "trophy wife."

"What a waste," Jake thought.

Eventually, they turned to discussing the rebellion at UAardvark. Although Jake was circumspect at first, he soon realized that he needn't be, for Mary Jo was a sympathizer. Delighted by the revolt's tactics, she also thoroughly approved of its goals. "Wisdom," she said, "shouldn't be reduced to a corporate commodity."

Finally, looking directly at him, she said: "I've enjoyed speaking with you, Jake, but, of course, as I'm sure you recognize, I've called you here to discuss something else."

Jake nodded.

"As I mentioned earlier tonight," she began, "Dwight isn't

around in the evenings. Indeed, he isn't around much at all. This fact, plus his general coolness toward me, made me very suspicious. So, some time ago, I hired a private detective to keep an eye on him, especially in the evenings."

She stopped for a time, but, then, continued. "Eventually, the detective concluded that Dwight was having an affair with a woman here in town. And he provided me with pictures he had taken that proved it."

"I'm sorry to hear that," Jake remarked.

"Well, it's not a disaster," she responded. "Some time ago, I concluded that I made a mistake in marrying him. After all," she said, smiling, "he's a juvenile, insensitive, coke-snorting, brainless idiot."

They both laughed at that.

"And I couldn't stand his old friends or those businessmen he was always hitting up for large financial contributions."

"Anyway," she said, "this is the proverbial last straw. I'm ending the marriage, although I have no desire to use this incident to sue Dwight for alimony or to drag him through the courts. Instead, what I'm planning to do is to move out of here right away and pay a short visit to my family in Connecticut. Then I'll relocate, maybe permanently, to Japan, where I'll study Buddhism. In fact, though Dwight doesn't know it yet, arrangements for my move to Japan have already been made."

"And where do I come into all of this?" asked Jake.

"Well," she said, "it occurred to me that you might find the pictures taken by my detective useful in your campaign to rid UAardvark of corporate influence—and certainly of Dwight."

Unsure how to respond, Jake finally said: "But Mary Jo,

this kind of personal stuff wouldn't be very effective in sparking popular outrage, on campus or in the nation. After all, half the people in the United States have had affairs at some time or other in their lives."

"This one might be more explosive, Jake," she said.

"Why do you think that?" he asked.

In response, she reached into a large manila folder and withdrew a picture, which she handed to him. "Feel free to use it in any way you'd like," she said.

The picture, in full color, showed Dwight Hopkins on his hands and knees, with his rear end exposed. Astride his back sat a gaunt women, dressed in black, with a cruel smile on her face. In her hand she held a small whip with which she was clearly beating his buttocks. The buttocks, in fact, looked fiery red. They strongly contrasted with the skin color of the woman, which was green.

# Chapter 38

## The Ultimate Scandal

The scandal broke the next morning, when the photo of Wilma ("The Witch") Welsh whipping President Dwight Hopkins's bare buttocks appeared on the front page of the *Aardvark Enterprise*, alongside a lengthy editorial calling upon Hopkins and other members of his administration to resign.

Mary Jo had been right. The information was too sensational for the mass media to resist. When Jake brought the photo to the downtown offices of the newspaper that night, the editor— long hesitant to ruffle the feathers of the Establishment— realized that he had the story and photo of the year in hand. And following their publication, the mass media immediately spread them all around the globe.

Although the *New York Times*, the last bastion of "dignified" journalism, refused to publish the photo, the image was soon the center of public discussion everywhere, as was the background information on previous events at UAardvark.

Fox News weighed in early with its interpretation. Rush Limbaugh warned that the exposé was probably part of a "feminazi sting operation, put together by the whores, sluts, and queers in the so-called Girl Scouts of America."

MSNBC, on the other hand, saw the scandal as proof that the Democrats would soon bring the Republican "war on the middle class" to an end. Its labor-friendly commentator, Ed Schultz, argued that Dwight Hopkins's disgrace was a harbinger of the Republicans' political demise.

Some public responses, of course, were favorable. In a press release, the Witchcraft Society of America stated that Dr. Wilma Welsh provided inspiration to all who practiced the ancient art, especially on the nation's campuses. President Hopkins, the statement insisted, was obviously an unusually tolerant, open-minded educator, unafraid to challenge the conventional wisdom.

Like many things, the scandal was also grist for the political mill. Asked for his comment on it, the U.S. Senate Republican leader declared that the nation's descent into immorality could be traced directly to the "secular liberalism" of the Democratic Party. The only solutions for it, he said, were deregulation of business and tax cuts for the wealthy.

When the Senate Democratic leader was asked for his thoughts on the scandal, he replied that it would never have occurred if the Republicans had joined the Democrats in making reasonable compromises.

For its part, the League of Revolutionary Peasants and Workers—despite being reduced to nine members after a split-off by a dissident faction (the Bolshevik Tendency)—issued a 17-page analysis of the situation and promised to send a representative to UAardvark to take charge of the campus struggle.

As usual, the public shrugged off all political pronouncements, but was eager to learn more about the scandal, particularly the exploits of what was now being termed "the dynamic duo."

Fully aware of this, hundreds of reporters fanned out throughout Aardvark and its environs, seeking to locate Dwight and Wilma for their comments or, better yet, pictures. But they had disappeared. Dwight was not at his campus office or at his home. Indeed, no one seemed to be at the presidential mansion, for Mary Jo Hopkins had flown the coop that morning. Nor was Wilma anywhere to be found.

Wilma's absence, though, coming on top of the growing campus turmoil and the latest scandal, led to the calling of an emergency meeting of the executive committee of United UAardvark Faculty. At the meeting, Wilma's critics charged that she had betrayed their trust by "sleeping with the enemy"— although, as the photos revealed, this did not quite describe her activity. And even Wilma's strongest supporters were now disenchanted with her behavior. As a result, the executive committee voted to remove her from office and, then, turned to electing a new union president. Convinced that an oppositional stance toward the administration was imperative, the executive committee proceeded to elect Gina Sorrentino to this post. In her first act as president, Gina proposed a resolution to declare UUF officially in support of the campus general strike. It passed unanimously.

Meanwhile, the Republican governor of Indiana, Engelbert Stupp, was pressed by the media to issue a statement in response to the latest scandal. In recent weeks, as the UAardvark campus had erupted in protest, he had been a staunch supporter of President Hopkins and "The Business-Friendly University." But, with Hopkins disgraced, it was time to do some fancy footwork. Consequently, after about an hour closeted with his political advisors, Governor Stupp emerged to hold a press conference at which he said that he had long harbored doubts about the university president's competence and mental stability. Although restrained, in the past, by his charitable and forgiving nature, he had now reluctantly concluded that the time had come to launch a thorough investigation of administration behavior at UAardvark.

The new scandal also had a considerable effect upon the UAardvark Board of Trustees. Previously, it had stood solidly behind Hopkins. But a number of the trustees, although happy enough with his pro-business efforts, were now convinced that he had outlived his usefulness. After all, since the uprising had begun, fundraising had fallen off, lawsuits were pouring in, publicity was terrible, and this new sex scandal undermined the prestige and credibility of the university with which they were associated.

As a result, a crisis session of the board of trustees opened that very afternoon. Several trustees leveled a blistering attack on Hopkins's leadership, arguing that almost anyone in the United States, and in many other countries, would be preferable to him as university president. But his fraternity buddies on the board fought back in his defense, while still other trustees felt that to abandon him in these circumstances would "play into the hands of the revolutionary rabble on the campus." Ultimately, then, the board decided on a compromise approach: supporting the governor's call for a full investigation of the administration's behavior.

By that evening, a perfect storm raged around the Hopkins-Welsh scandal and around the broader issues raised by the administration's policy at UAardvark. At colleges and universities around the nation, demonstrations erupted, demanding the replacement of administrators with worker-student councils. The mass media gave the issues, or at least some of them, blanket coverage. Politicians prated about the decline of higher education. Polls showed that 83 percent of the public thought that Hopkins should resign and that 64 percent thought corporate interests should be reined in on college and university campuses.

When Hopkins—hiding with Wilma in his secret bunker, located alongside the New Technology Center—phoned his fraternity brothers on the board of trustees that evening, they gave him a pessimistic report.

"We barely held the line today, old buddy," said one. "So I'd say it's time to split."

Another sought to soften the blow: "You've got plenty of money socked away in the Caymans, Dwight. Why not take off for some exotic island paradise and enjoy yourself? And you can bring along that, uh, woman friend of yours, too." He stopped for a moment, then continued, using another football metaphor from the good old college days of hard drinking and hard playing. "Dwight," he said, "the time has come for you to punt."

# Chapter 39

## The Revolution Triumphant

On the following day, shortly before eight in the morning, a large elevator brought a luxury automobile, styled as a racing car, up from President Hopkins's secret underground bunker. Dwight and Wilma sat upright in the front seats, while minimal luggage and numerous codes to access the campus president's substantial overseas financial holdings were locked in the trunk. When they arrived at the surface, Hopkins pressed a button, and a cleverly camouflaged outer door slid open silently. Looking furtively both ways, he gunned the auto's powerful engine and, then, roared off across the campus and out its gates. At that hour, few were awake to observe Dwight and Wilma's departure. Nor did they tell anyone their destination.

As the car careened across the campus, however, an alert photographer, camped out on a lawn, snapped a photo that, when enlarged, clearly showed who the passengers were. Within minutes, the picture was being transmitted to the mass media and to the world. On television, radio, and the Internet, pundits announced that the embattled university president and his strange dominatrix had fled, or, as some said, "abdicated."

In response, celebrations erupted on numerous college and university campuses. At UAardvark, on the newly-named Social Justice Plaza (formerly Commerce Plaza), a mass meeting convened. Within short order, attendees decided that the moment had arrived to sweep away the vestiges of the administrative façade. In a nearly unanimous vote, members of the university community agreed to seize and occupy the offices of the administration.

When thousands of faculty, students, professional staff, and blue-collar workers arrived at the offices, they found that most were already vacant. But, in those few that were still occupied, they simply told the vice presidents, associate vice presidents, assistant vice presidents, and assorted deans to clear out, which, in these new circumstances, the administrators quickly did. It was not at all difficult to enter offices that had been either abandoned or occupied, for the cleaning staff had the keys to all of them.

As in many social upheavals, the revolutionaries were looking forward to discovering interesting things in the records of the old regime. In this regard, however, they were initially disappointed. The file cabinets abandoned by administrators were stuffed with completed surveys that no one had read, student evaluation forms, official memos that were too illiterate and banal to be endured, bottles of liquor, and commercial brochures that advertised hair dyes, wrinkle-removers, and cures for erectile dysfunction. Although there were numerous bookshelves, few held any books.

When the rebels arrived at the office of President Hopkins, a smiling Marsha Skelton came out to greet them. After giving them a little tour of the place, she turned them loose on the records. Here the materials were more interesting, for the records included hefty files on all faculty and staff members, apparently developed with the assistance of the FBI, university agents, and other investigative bodies. In addition, aside from the same sort of items turned up elsewhere, there was a collection of miniature racing cars, a small supply of cocaine, and an assortment of pornographic magazines, videos, and DVDs. Computer-savvy activists also had high hopes of finding interesting material on the former president's hard drive, which they now carted off for a more thorough examination at the university IT center.

After a quick lunch, prepared and served by volunteers on the lawn, the university's new Workers and Students Council formally proclaimed the ouster of the Hopkins administration and constituted itself the university's new governing body. In this context, it announced that the general strike, having been successful in overturning the Old Order, had now come to an end.

For a time, the council debated the wisdom of having any administrative officers at the university. Deciding, however, that a chief executive officer could be useful for maintaining the physical plant and keeping records, the council elected Marsha Skelton university president. She promised that she would exercise very limited power in university affairs, simply seeing to it that the garbage was collected, the floors were swept, the electricity was restored, and the mail was delivered. Well pleased with this plan but wary of returning to an executive tyranny, the council announced that it would review her contract after one year.

Turning to other pressing matters, the Workers and Students Council voted to eliminate 90 percent of the administrative posts and to lower the salaries of the remainder to the average salary for faculty members. Thanks to the enormous savings that would be realized on administrative costs, the council decided to raise the salaries of blue-collar workers to the faculty/administration level. Some council members, in fact, argued that, as the cleaning and dining-halls staff worked harder than did faculty and administrators, their pay should be higher. But most council members felt that maintaining the principle of equality outweighed that consideration.

Students, particularly, were anxious to end soaring tuition costs and pressed for the abolition of tuition. Everyone thought that would be a good idea. However, as it was not yet clear to what extent the university could maintain itself without students picking up some of the cost, it was decided that tuition would be cut by 50 percent per year until revenue fell to a level beyond which campus operations would be jeopardized.

The council also took action in other areas that had long been a matter of concern to the campus community. All corporate and military connections were proclaimed terminated. These included the arrangements for the New Technology Center. As that building had been almost completed, the council decided to close the Tunnels and turn the center into a workshop and communal living space for the cleaning and maintenance workers.

As for the television sets, they would be immediately removed from classroom buildings, dorms, and other university structures and brought to the New Technology Center, where they would be refashioned by the maintenance crews into toilet bowls.

\* \* \*

That same afternoon, as these dramatic changes were occurring at UAardvark, William T. Swagger V and General Buck Thorkelson conferred via one of the Pentagon's secure phone lines.

"Well, it looks like that idiot, that @^$*&% Hopkins, has blown it," Swagger snorted with disgust. "The game is lost. Even J. Edgar has thrown in the towel and pulled the FBI out of its investigation of UAardvark. I should have known Hopkins wasn't up to the job." He paused to sneak a quick peek at his net worth.

"Yes, it's too bad he proved so weak," said Thorkelson. "If it were up to me, I would have taken those ^)*^$#^% campus queers out and shot them. Anyway, it's too late for that now. About all that's left for us at this point is to begin damage control."

"What do you recommend?" asked Swagger.

"Well, the nuclear waste storage plan at UAardvark is definitely dead. Maybe we can find some gullible administrators on another campus. Why don't you check out some of those southern Bible colleges? Meanwhile, of course, I'll deny any connection to nuclear waste at UAardvark. And I'll see to it that Hopkins is captured and, then, secretly placed in a well-secured room with three television sets blasting away continuously for the next quarter century. That should take care of whatever is left of his brain."

"And what about Wilma—the witch?" Swagger asked.

The general's face flushed. "Oh, I'm going to offer her a job down here in Washington," he said. "I could always use another secretary. She'll either accept it or get locked up in a room like Hopkins."

"But why are you interested in employing her, Buck?"

"Well, it's a long story," the general remarked, with a sigh. "But what it comes down to is that I kinda like her style. And I wonder what those green feet would look like around the office."

# Chapter 40

## A Martyr for the Cause?

In the late afternoon, as news of the sweeping changes at UAardvark spread throughout the university, thousands of people gathered on Social Justice Plaza for a wild celebration.

The vast crowd—composed of faculty, students, professional staff, blue-collar workers, police, journalists, and curious onlookers—joined in joyous singing, dancing, and drumming. From a makeshift stage, hulking Hells Angels motorcyclists contributed their poetry, including a special haiku written for the occasion by The Crusher:

We move yet closer
To the great transformation
When we all are free.

Between cultural performances, speakers regaled the crowd with news of the decisions made by the Workers and Students Council. Each decision was received with thunderous cheers, especially the ones stripping the administration of almost all its powers and terminating university connections with corporations and the military.

Messages of congratulation poured in from all over the nation and the world.

"You are lighting the way to the future," said the Student-Worker Alliance of the University of Tokyo.

"We need neither robber-baron capitalists nor repressive

commissars," proclaimed the Democratic Alliance of the University of Moscow.

From the University of Kansas, a group calling itself Populist Renewal declared: "In the tradition of our courageous forebears, we promise to raise less corn and more hell."

One rather mixed message was received from the League of Revolutionary Peasants and Workers, which promised that its representative would soon arrive to correct the ideological errors of UAardvark activists and to take charge of the situation on their campus. This proved a source of much amusement to the crowd.

News also began to flow in about groups taking action elsewhere. At Michigan State University, the faculty senate voted to cancel all contracts with corporations. Refusing to accept any further directives from the Vassar College administration, faculty and students drove it off campus. At Duke University, the underpaid maintenance, food-service, and cleaning workers got together and declared a general strike. In Peking, irate students and faculty at the university threw the campus president head first into a pile of manure.

Meanwhile, 100 yards away from the UAardvark crowd, an armed patrol of camouflage-clad Christian Patriots observed the gathering anxiously from a grassy knoll.

As usual, confusion reigned. The Rev. Billy Ray Jones, hearing the messages from groups in foreign lands, concluded that un-American activities must be afoot, although he couldn't figure out what they were. For his part, Stan Slobodov continued to argue that the real problem could be traced to "uppity women." In justification for this position, he pointed to the choice of Marsha as the new university president. But, although wavering, the others were not convinced. Everyone in the group was pleased by the departure of Hopkins, who they assumed (incorrectly) was a Jew. Even so, as Hopkins was now out of the picture, they lacked a handy enemy—unless, of course, the Muslims were involved. But where were they?

On stage, the speeches were in full flower. Tom, quoting Marx, claimed that, in this country and abroad, the proletariat was growing increasingly restless. "The day of working-class liberation," he promised, "is coming ever closer." Speaking for UUF, Gina gave a rabble-rousing defense of the rights of all campus workers. Concluding, she raised her fist and proclaimed: "An injury to one is an injury to all!"

Following Gina, Natasha took the stage. With her purple hair ablaze in the sunlight, she began: "Students and workers! We have stood together in this campaign! And we will continue to stand together!" A roar erupted from the crowd. "Yes, this is the beginning of the struggle—not the end. The hardest part has only begun. And that is building for ourselves and the world a model of what a democratic university can be—a university not designed for corporate profit, but to light the way forward for humanity. Solidarity forever!"

It was hard to top that, but Jake, the next speaker, was at his most eloquent. This, plus the fact that, by this point, most people on campus knew of his central role in the upheaval, led the gathering to cheer fervently as he whipped up the excitement.

Even from their more remote location, the Christian Patriots sensed his importance and listened carefully, if without much comprehension, to what he said.

"It's that troublemaker Jake Holland again," complained Colonel Bumpkin. "We've been suspicious of him for some time. And with that dark skin, he certainly looks like a Muslim to me."

Private McNamara, the FBI infiltrator in the group, did his best to dissuade the Christian Patriot leader. "I don't think so, colonel," he remarked. Actually, thanks to FBI briefings on the UAardvark situation, McNamara knew that Jake was Jewish. But he figured that, if he mentioned this fact, it would inflame the lunatic colonel even more.

"Men, ready your rifles," said Colonel Bumpkin.

McNamara began sweating. It would look really bad if the Christian Patriots did something crazy while on his watch. A major setback for his career. "&##&*^$!" he told himself. "What's wrong with these people?"

Meanwhile, Jake continued to stir the crowd. "Decent universities," he proclaimed, "don't need *meshuga* administrators and corporate *goniffs*."

"There, you see," swore Colonel Bumpkin, his eyes narrowing to slits. "He's using A-rab lingo. Everything's clear now."

"No, no," retorted McNamara. "That's Yiddish. It means crazy administrators and corporate thieves." Sweating yet harder, he glanced around frantically for confirmation. But he wasn't going to get it from this gang.

"Yeah, Yiddish," said the Rev. Jones. "One of them Muslim languages."

"You said it, rev'rend," Colonel Bumpkin declared

enthusiastically, now convinced of the way forward. "Men: ready, aim—"

"Wait!" shouted McNamara.

"Fire!"

Five guns blazed.

Shouts and screams came from the crowd.

And Jake's body crumpled to the stage, covered with blood.

# Chapter 41

# The Political Is Personal

Jake awoke slowly in a hospital room. Some parts of him hurt, and others felt numb. Opening his eyes, he saw Ellen sitting by his bed, looking lovely and smiling fondly at him.

"I guess I'm not dead," he remarked. "Though maybe I'm in heaven."

"No, Jake, you're not," she said, taking his hand in her own. "You were wounded by three bullets, and they drew a lot of blood. But they didn't hit any vital organs. So, all things considered, you're in remarkably good shape."

"Was anyone else hurt?" he asked.

"No," she replied. "No one else was injured. Your assailants were apparently gunning for you alone."

"But why were they shooting at *me*?" he asked, dazed by the whole thing. "What was going on?"

Ellen began to laugh. But, then, considering it inappropriate in the circumstances, she stopped. "Believe it or not," she said, "you were attacked by a rightwing nut group called the Christian Patriots. They thought you were leading a Muslim takeover of the university—or maybe the United States, or maybe both!" Now she did laugh.

Jake started to laugh too. Noticing that it hurt, though, he quickly sobered up. "Well, I've been accused of lots of things," he said, "but never of organizing Muslim conspiracies. Anyway, what happened to the attackers?"

"Oh, they didn't come out of things well at all. Right after the shooting, your Hells Angels friends charged up the hill, grabbed them, and beat the hell out of them! One of those `Patriots,' who calls himself a `colonel,' was roughed up so badly by two of those motorcycle women—at least I think they were women—that he'll probably be in the hospital for a lot longer than you are. Meanwhile, all of the `Patriots' involved have been arrested and charged with attempted murder."

"Well, I guess that's the sorry fate of patriots these days," Jake joked, wincing a bit.

Looking worried at this sudden sign of pain, Ellen asked: "Should I have the nurse get you something to make you more comfortable?"

"No, it's OK," he said. "It's no worse than I used to feel some mornings when I woke up with a hangover!"

They both smiled, enjoying the recollection of what now seemed a very distant past.

"But how are you doing these days?" Jake asked. "Are you still looking for teaching jobs at other schools?"

"No, as a matter of fact," she said. "In response to a demand by the UAardvark Workers and Students Council, my firing from the university has been rescinded by the trustees, as have the other policies of the Hopkins administration. So, in these circumstances, I'm definitely staying here."

"That's fantastic!" exulted Jake. "I couldn't be happier." And he meant it. "If we had a bottle of champagne, I'd propose a toast—if I still drank, that is."

"And what about the bewitched Hopkins and Wilma?" he added. "Is there any sign of them?"

"No, none at all," Ellen responded. "No one knows where

they've gone, and there's no indication that they're planning to return."

"Well, good riddance," Jake said. "The university is certainly better off without them, and without those damned corporations."

"Oh, it's absolutely great these days," Ellen responded. "UAardvark has become such an exciting place. People are suddenly exchanging ideas all over the campus, and learning things they never did before. And new thinking is bubbling up not only around here, but also at colleges and universities around the world."

"Yes, it's pretty amazing," he said. "Of course, who knows how many of these changes can be sustained? But even if we don't reach utopia—and I'd be an idiot if I believed that we could—the groundwork has been laid for a better future."

Ellen nodded happily. "That's for certain. The corporate educational system and its former enthusiasts are retreating fast." Then, smiling, she added: "And that's largely thanks to you, Jake. You should be proud of yourself."

Embarrassed, Jake said: "Well, I'd like to claim credit for everything that's happened. But the reality is that the campaign to reclaim the university has been a collective effort. And it continues to be. I'm just a small part of the struggle."

"OK, it has been a collective effort," she conceded. "But you played the central role in it. Everyone knows that, including those lunatics who tried to kill you."

Ellen paused, embarrassed at what she was about to say. Finally, looking straight at him, she declared: "Jake, I want to own up to the fact that I made a terrible mistake. I misjudged you. I should have realized that under your burnt-out, cynical exterior, fires of resistance continued to rage. I'm sorry." Tears trickled down her cheeks, and she sought, unsuccessfully, to brush them away.

For a moment, Jake didn't know what to say. And then he did. "Does that mean that I'm no longer in the doghouse?" he asked.

"Don't be silly, Jake," she responded. "You were never in the doghouse. I always loved you. I just didn't think things would work out between us."

"And now?" he asked, pressing the point.

In reply, Ellen smiled at him mysteriously. Then she bent over and, pressing herself against his chest, kissed him on the lips, deeply and passionately.

Unfortunately, because of Jake's wounds, the embrace hurt. But it also felt wonderful, just as he knew it would. So he hung on to her, determined to never let her go.

# Memorandum #368

From: The Bureau of Knowledge

To:      All Learners

Re:      Educational Reform on the Backward Planet ("Earth")

Date:  7 Helios 31,058

We hope you have enjoyed learning more about educational reform among the Earthians from this latest Knowledge Expander.

As you ponder these unusual developments or discuss them with other Vartanians, we urge you to give some thought to the following questions, which—despite the attempts at explanations by the Earthian author—our Vartanian specialists continue to puzzle over:

Why are the Earthians prone to saying #$*&%^@ or its equivalent?

Why do individual Earthians covet billions of dollars?

Why do Earthians mate in such strange ways?

Who are the *goyim*?

Do not hesitate to send any thoughts you might have on these matters to the Bureau of Knowledge (knowledge@globalhappiness.edu).

Please be advised that unauthorized duplication or transmission of this Knowledge Expander will result in an investigation by the Federal Bureau of Inquisitions, and that such misbehavior will be subject to the full penalty of the law.

Did we startle you with that last statement? Don't worry about it. We're just making what the Earthians call a joke. Why would any reasonable creature want to impede the flow of knowledge?

Happy learning to all!

Born in Brooklyn, New York, Lawrence S. Wittner attended Columbia College, the University of Wisconsin, and Columbia University, where he received his Ph.D. in history. Subsequently, he taught at Hampton Institute, Vassar College, Japanese universities (under the Fulbright program), and at SUNY/Albany. An award-winning author, he has written nine books, edited or coedited another four, and written hundreds of published articles and book reviews. He also has been a long-time political activist, particularly in the peace, labor, and racial equality movements. Currently, he serves as executive secretary of the Albany County Central Federation of Labor, AFL-CIO and as a national board member of Peace Action. Further information about his life and activities can be found in his memoirs (*Working for Peace and Justice*) and on his website (www.lawrenceswittner.com). He can be contacted at: wittner@albany.edu.